1966 by The Reader's Digest Association, Inc.
1966 by The Reader's Digest Association (Canada) Ltd.

 e Digest and the Pegasus logo are registered trademarks of
 r Association, Inc.

 a this volume has been created by
 r Association, Inc.

 .

 CIATION WITH MEDIA PROJECTS INCORPORATED

 ter Smith
 anette Mall
 eline Ogburn
 rles Wills
 Elizabeth Prince
 d Schleifer

 Catalog Number: 88-63376
 2-9

 s published and distributed by Choice Publishing, Inc.,
 021, with permission of The Reader's Digest Association, Inc.

 e United States of America.

 2

R

BEST LOVE
FOR YOUNC

Great C
Sherlock

A SELECTION AND C

Storie
Sir Arthur Co

Illustrated by

CHOICE PUBLIS

New Yo

PRODUCED IN AS

Executive Editor,
Managing Editor,
Project Editor, Jac
Associate Editor, C
Contributing Edito
Art Director, Ber

Library of Congr
ISBN: 0-945260

This 1989 editio
Great Neck, NY

Manufactured in

10 9 8 7 6 5

Foreword

SHERLOCK HOLMES, the incomparable detective created by Sir Arthur Conan Doyle, has thrilled and delighted four generations of readers. Now a new generation is reveling in this extraordinary gentleman's ability to get at the truth from the slightest of clues, to protect the innocent from mysterious strangers, and to bring the cleverest of criminals to justice.

Holmes's adventures, of which eight of the best are presented here, were once described by the late Christopher Morley as "pure anesthesia." "Unquestionably," wrote Mr. Morley, "there is poppy in these tales. As we enter Holmes's sitting room at 221B Baker Street, we are lifted out of ourselves into the world of Victorian London, a world of high-wheeled hansom cabs and curling fog, in which Holmes performs uncanny feats of detection while we (and his faithful friend, Dr. Watson) look on with amazement."

Conan Doyle was born in Edinburgh, Scotland, in 1859, the eldest son of a distinguished artist. He had, like his famous fictional hero, a scientific turn of mind; and, after taking his medical degree at the Royal Infirmary in Edinburgh, he went to London to begin the practice of medicine. Like the Dr. Watson of his stories, he had leisure time between patients, and he used this time to apply his keen powers of observation and reasoning, his lively humor and imagination to writing stories.

A Study in Scarlet, his first published work (from which is taken the Prologue of the present collection), appeared in 1887. When *The Adventures of Sherlock Holmes* first started to appear in *The Strand* magazine in 1891, they were immediately and immensely popular. However, despite the public's boundless enthusiasm for the Holmes stories, Conan Doyle's main interest lay with the historical novel, of which he produced some justifiably popular examples—among them *Micah Clarke, The White Company*, and *Rodney Stone*. But it was his success with Sherlock Holmes that enabled him to turn to writing full time.

When the Boer War broke out, he served in South Africa as a senior medical officer. And in his capacity as a writer, he defended British policy in two books, *The Great Boer War* and *The War in South Africa: Its Causes and Conduct*. For these services to his country he was knighted in 1902. During World War I he was to give again of his talents, writing propaganda for the Allies. His *Cause and Conduct of the World War* was published in twelve languages besides English.

In his later years he became deeply interested in spiritualism. With the same wholehearted enthusiasm as he had poured into his earlier interests, he lectured widely on this subject and wrote a two-volume *History of Spiritualism*. Sir Arthur Conan Doyle died in 1930 at the age of seventy-one. But his own gallant spirit is very much abroad as Sherlock Holmes rushes with a cool head and a generous heart into one ominous tangle of mystery after another, taking Dr. Watson—and the eager reader—along with him.

Contents

Prologue

Being a Reprint from
the Reminiscences of John H. Watson, M.D.,
Late of the Army Medical Department.

IN THE YEAR 1878 I took my degree of doctor of medicine at the University of London, and proceeded to Netley to go through the course prescribed for surgeons in the Army. Having completed my studies there, I was duly attached to the Fifth Northumberland Fusiliers as assistant surgeon. The regiment was stationed in India, and by the time I entered upon my new duties the Second Afghan War had broken out.

For me the campaign brought nothing but misfortune and disaster. At the battle of Maiwand, I was struck on the shoulder by a jezail bullet, which shattered the bone and grazed the subclavian artery. Worn with pain, I was removed to the base hospital at Peshawar. Here I had already improved so far as to be able to walk about the wards, when I was struck down by enteric fever, that curse of our Indian possessions. When at last I became convalescent, I was so weak and emaciated that I was sent back to England.

I had neither kith nor kin in England, and was therefore as free as an income of eleven shillings and sixpence a day will permit a man to be. I stayed for some time at a private hotel in London, leading a meaningless existence, and spending money more freely than I ought. So alarming did the state of my finances become, that I soon realized that I must take up my quarters in some less pretentious and less expensive domicile.

On the very day that I had come to this conclusion, I was standing at the Criterion Bar, when someone tapped me on the shoulder, and turning round I recognized young Stamford, who had been a dresser under me at Barts. I asked him to lunch with me at the Holborn, and we started off in a hansom.

"Whatever have you been doing with yourself, Watson?" he asked in undisguised wonder, as we rattled through the crowded London streets. "You are as thin as a lath and as brown as a nut."

I gave him a short sketch of my adventures. "And now," I concluded when we reached our destination, "I'm trying to solve the problem as to whether it is possible to get comfortable rooms at a reasonable price."

"That's a strange thing. You are the second man today who has used that expression to me," remarked my companion. "A fellow who is working at the chemical laboratory up at the hospital was bemoaning himself this morning because he could not get someone to go halves with him in some nice rooms which he had found, and which were too much for his purse."

"By Jove!" I cried. "I am the very man for him. I should prefer having a partner to being alone."

Young Stamford looked rather strangely at me over his wineglass. "You don't know Sherlock Holmes," he said; "perhaps you would not care for him as a constant companion. He is a little queer in his ideas—an enthusiast in some branches of science."

"A medical student, I suppose?" said I.

"No—he is well up in anatomy, and he is a first-class chemist; but he has never taken any systematic medical classes. His studies are very desultory and eccentric, but he has amassed a lot of out-of-the-way knowledge which would astonish his professors."

"If I am to lodge with anyone," I said, "I should prefer a man of studious and quiet habits. I am not strong enough yet to stand much noise or excitement. How could I meet your friend?"

"He is sure to be at the laboratory," returned my companion. "He either avoids the place for weeks, or else he works there from morning till night. We can drive round together after luncheon." And the conversation drifted away into other channels.

As we made our way to the hospital after leaving the Holborn, Stamford gave me a few more particulars about the gentleman whom I proposed to take as a fellow lodger.

"Holmes is a little too scientific for my tastes," he said with a laugh. "I could imagine his giving a friend a little pinch of the latest vegetable alkaloid, not out of malevolence, you understand, but simply out of a spirit of inquiry in order to have an accurate idea of the effects. To do him justice, I think that he would take it himself with the same readiness. But here we are, and you must form your own impressions about him." We turned down a narrow lane and passed through a small side door, which opened into a wing of the great hospital.

The chemical laboratory was a lofty chamber, lined and littered with countless bottles. Broad, low tables were scattered about, which bristled with retorts, test tubes, and little Bunsen burners, with their flickering blue flames. There was only one student in the room, who was bending over a distant table absorbed in his work. At the sound of our steps he glanced round and sprang to his feet with a cry of pleasure.

"I've found it! I've found it," he shouted, running towards us with a test tube in his hand. "I have found a reagent which is precipitated by hemoglobin, and by nothing else."

"Dr. Watson, Mr. Sherlock Holmes," said Stamford.

"How are you?" Holmes said cordially, gripping my hand with a strength for which I should hardly have given him credit. "You have been in Afghanistan, I perceive."

"How on earth did you know that?" I asked in astonishment.

"Never mind," said he, chuckling to himself. "The question now is about hemoglobin. No doubt you see the significance of this discovery of mine?"

"It is interesting chemically, no doubt," I answered, "but practically—"

"Why, man, it is the most practical medicolegal discovery for years. Come over here now!" He seized me by the coat sleeve in his eagerness, and drew me over to the table at which he had been working. "Let us have some fresh blood," he said, digging a long

3

bodkin into his finger, and drawing off the resulting drop of blood in a chemical pipette. "Now, I add this small quantity of blood to a liter of water. You perceive that the resulting mixture has the appearance of pure water. The proportion of blood cannot be more than one in a million. I have no doubt, however, that we shall be able to obtain the characteristic reaction." As he spoke, he threw into the vessel a few white crystals, and then added some drops of a transparent fluid. In an instant the contents assumed a dull mahogany color, and a brownish dust was precipitated to the bottom of the glass jar.

"Ha! Ha!" he cried, clapping his hands, and looking as delighted as a child with a new toy. "What do you think of that?"

"It seems to be a very delicate test," I remarked.

"Beautiful! Beautiful! Criminal cases are continually hinging upon that one point. A man is suspected of a crime months perhaps after it has been committed. His linen or clothes are examined and brownish stains discovered upon them. Are they blood stains, or mud stains, or rust stains, or fruit stains, or what are they? That is the question which has puzzled many an expert, and why? Because there was no reliable test. Now we have the Sherlock Holmes test, and there will no longer be any difficulty."

His eyes fairly glittered as he spoke, and he put his hand over his heart and bowed as if to some applauding crowd conjured up by his imagination.

"We came here on business," said Stamford, sitting down on a high three-legged stool, and pushing another one in my direction with his foot. "My friend here wants to take diggings; and I thought that I had better bring you together."

Holmes seemed delighted at the idea of sharing his rooms with me. "I have my eye on a suite in Baker Street," he said, "which would suit us down to the ground. I generally have chemicals about, and occasionally do experiments. Would that annoy you?"

"By no means."

"Let me see—what are my other shortcomings? I get in the dumps at times, and don't open my mouth for days on end. You must not think I am sulky when I do that. Just let me alone, and

I'll soon be right. What have you to confess now? It's just as well for two fellows to know the worst of one another before they begin to live together."

I laughed at this cross-examination. "I keep a bull pup," I said, "and I object to noise, because my nerves are shaken, and I am extremely lazy. I have another set of vices when I'm well, but those are the principal ones at present."

"Oh, that's all right," he cried, with a merry laugh. "I think we can consider the thing as settled—that is if the rooms are agreeable to you."

"When shall we see them?"

"Call for me here at noon tomorrow, and we'll go together to see them."

"All right—noon exactly," said I, shaking his hand.

We left him working among his chemicals, and we walked together towards my hotel. "By the way," I asked suddenly, stopping and turning upon Stamford, "how the deuce did he know that I had come from Afghanistan?"

My companion smiled an enigmatical smile. "That's just his little peculiarity," he said. "A good many people have wanted to know how he finds things out."

"Oh! A mystery is it?" I cried, rubbing my hands. "This is very piquant. I am much obliged to you for bringing us together. 'The proper study of mankind is man,' you know."

"You must study him, then," Stamford said, as he bade me good-by. "You'll find him a knotty problem, though."

"Good-by," I answered, and strolled on to my hotel, considerably interested in my new acquaintance.

WE MET NEXT DAY AND INSPECTED the rooms at No. 221B Baker Street. They consisted of a couple of comfortable bedrooms and a single large airy sitting room, cheerfully furnished, and illuminated by two broad windows. So desirable were the apartments, and so moderate did the terms seem when divided between us, that the bargain was concluded upon the spot.

That very evening I moved my things round from the hotel, and

on the following morning Sherlock Holmes followed me with several boxes and portmanteaus. In the succeeding days I found that he was certainly not a difficult man to live with. He was quiet in his ways, and his habits were regular. Sometimes he spent his day at the chemical laboratory, sometimes in the dissecting rooms, and occasionally in long walks, which appeared to take him into the lowest portions of the City. Nothing could exceed his energy when the working fit was upon him; but now and again a reaction would seize him, and for days on end he would lie upon the sofa in the sitting room, hardly uttering a word or moving a muscle from morning to night.

As the weeks went by, my interest in him deepened and increased. His very person and appearance were such as to strike the attention of the most casual observer. In height he was rather over six feet, and so excessively lean that he seemed to be considerably taller. His eyes were sharp and piercing, save during those intervals of torpor to which I have alluded; and his thin, hawklike nose gave his whole expression an air of alertness and decision. His chin, too, had the prominence and squareness which mark the man of determination. The reader may set me down as a hopeless busybody, when I confess how much this man stimulated my curiosity, and how often I endeavored to break through the reticence which he showed on all that concerned himself. Before pronouncing judgment, however, be it remembered how objectless was my life, and how little there was to engage my attention.

During the first week or so we had no callers, and I had begun to think that my companion was as friendless a man as I was myself. Presently, however, I found that he had many acquaintances, and those in the most different classes of society. One morning a young girl called, fashionably dressed, and stayed for half an hour or more. The same afternoon brought a gray-headed, seedy visitor, looking like a peddler. On another occasion an old white-haired gentleman had an interview with my companion; and on another, a railway porter in his velveteen uniform. When any of these individuals put in an appearance, Sherlock Holmes used to beg for the use of the sitting room, and I would retire to my bedroom. He always apologized to me for putting me to this inconvenience. "I have to use this room as a place of business," he said, "and these people are my clients." My delicacy prevented me from asking him a point-blank question, but he soon came round to the subject of his own accord.

It was upon the fourth of March, as I remember, that I rose somewhat earlier than usual, and found that Sherlock Holmes had not yet finished his breakfast. I picked up a magazine from the table in the sitting room and attempted to while away the time with it while Mrs. Hudson, our housekeeper, was preparing my coffee. One of the articles had a pencil mark at the heading. I began to run my eye through it.

It attempted to show how much an observant man might learn by an accurate and systematic examination of all that came in his way. The writer claimed by a momentary expression, a twitch of a muscle or a glance of an eye, to fathom a man's inmost thoughts. "The Science of Deduction and Analysis is one which can only be acquired by long and patient study," said the writer. "Let the inquirer begin by mastering elementary problems. Let him, on meeting a fellow mortal, learn at a glance to distinguish the history of the man, and the trade or profession to which he belongs. Such an exercise sharpens the faculties of observation, and teaches one where to look and what to look for. By a man's fingernails, by his boots, by his trouser knees, by the callosities of his forefinger and thumb, by his expression—by each of these things a man's calling is revealed."

"What ineffable twaddle!" I cried, slapping the magazine down on the table. "I see, Holmes, that you have read this article since you have marked it. It is evidently the theory of some armchair lounger who evolves all these neat little paradoxes in the seclusion of his own study. It is not practical. I should like to see him clapped down in a third-class carriage on the Underground, and asked to give the trades of all his fellow travelers. I would lay a thousand to one against him."

"You would lose your money," Holmes remarked calmly. "As for the article, I wrote it myself."

"You!"

"Yes. The theories which appear to you to be so chimerical are really extremely practical—so practical that I depend upon them for my bread and cheese."

"And how?" I asked involuntarily.

"Well, I have a trade of my own. I suppose I am the only one in the world. I'm a consulting detective. Here in London we have lots of government detectives and lots of private ones. When these fellows are at fault, they come to me, and I manage to put them on the right scent. They lay all the evidence before me, and I am generally able, by the help of my knowledge of the history of crime, to set them straight. There is a strong family resemblance about misdeeds, and if you have the details of a thousand at your finger ends, it is odd if you can't unravel the thousand and first. Other people are sent by private agencies. They are all in trouble about something, and want enlightening. I listen to their story, they listen to my comments, and then I pocket my fee."

"But do you mean to say," I said, "that without leaving your rooms you can unravel some knot which other men can make nothing of, although they have seen every detail for themselves?"

"Quite so. I have a kind of intuition that way. Now and again a case turns up which is a little more complex. Then I have to bustle about and see things with my own eyes. Observation with me is second nature. You appeared to be surprised when I told you, on our first meeting, that you had come from Afghanistan."

"You were told, no doubt."

"Nothing of the sort. I *knew* you came from Afghanistan. The train of reasoning ran, Here is a gentleman of a medical type, but with the air of a military man. Clearly an Army doctor, then. He has just come from the tropics, for his face is dark, and that is not the natural tint of his skin, for his wrists are fair. He has undergone hardship and sickness, as his haggard face says clearly. His left arm has been injured. He holds it in a stiff, unnatural manner. Where in the tropics could an English Army doctor have seen much hardship and got his arm wounded? Clearly in Afghanistan. The whole train of thought did not occupy a second. I then remarked that you came from Afghanistan, and you were astonished."

"It is simple enough as you explain it," I said, smiling.

Once Dr. Watson understood the nature of Holmes's work, he became his faithful helper and the chronicler of their shared adventures. The following are among the case histories recorded by Dr. Watson during the years he and Holmes shared lodgings, and afterwards when Watson married and set up in medical practice.

IT WAS A COLD MORNING in early spring, and we sat after breakfast on either side of a cheery fire in the sitting room in Baker Street. A thick fog rolled down between the lines of dun-colored houses, and the opposing windows loomed like dark, shapeless blurs through the heavy yellow wreaths. Our gas was lit, and shone on the white cloth and glimmer of china and metal, for Mrs. Hudson had not yet cleared the table.

"Man, or at least criminal man, has lost all enterprise and originality," Holmes remarked, as he sat puffing at his long cherry-wood pipe and gazing down into the fire. "As to my own little practice, it seems to be degenerating into an agency for recovering lost lead pencils and giving advice to young ladies from boarding schools. This note I had this morning marks my zero point, I fancy. Read it!"

He tossed a crumpled letter across to me. It was dated the preceding evening, and ran thus:

> Dear Mr. Holmes,
>
> I am very anxious to consult you as to whether I should or should not accept a situation which has been offered to me as governess. I shall call at half past ten tomorrow, if I do not inconvenience you.
>
> Yours faithfully,
> Violet Hunter

"Do you know the young lady?" I asked.

"Not I. But it is half past ten now, and I have no doubt that is her ring."

"It may turn out to be of more interest than you think."

As I spoke the door opened, and a young lady entered the room.

She was plainly but neatly dressed, with a bright, quick face, freckled like a plover's egg, and with the brisk manner of a woman who has had her own way to make in the world.

"You will excuse my troubling you, I am sure," said she, as my companion rose to greet her; "but I have had a very strange experience, and as I have no parents or relations of any sort from whom I could ask advice, I thought that perhaps you would be kind enough to tell me what I should do."

"Pray take a seat, Miss Hunter. I shall be happy to do anything that I can to serve you."

I could see that Holmes was favorably impressed by the manner and speech of his new client. He looked her over in his searching fashion, and then composed himself, with his lids drooping and his fingertips together, to listen to her story.

"I have been a governess for five years," said she, "in the family of Colonel Spence Munro, but two months ago the colonel went over to America with his children, so that I was without a situation.

"There is a well-known agency for governesses in the West End where I have been calling about once a week. It is managed by Miss Stoper. She sits in her own little office, and the ladies seeking employment wait in an anteroom, and are shown in one by one.

"Well, when I called last week I was shown into the little office but I found that Miss Stoper was not alone. A prodigiously stout man with a smiling face, and a great heavy chin which rolled down in fold upon fold over his throat, sat at her elbow. As I came in he looked at me and gave quite a jump in his chair, and turned quickly to Miss Stoper.

"'That will do,' said he. 'I could not ask for anything better. Capital! Capital!' He seemed quite enthusiastic and rubbed his hands together in the most genial fashion.

"'You are looking for a situation as governess, miss?' he asked.

"'Yes, sir.'

"'And what salary do you ask?'

"'I had four pounds a month in my last place.'

"'Oh, tut-tut!' he cried, throwing his fat hands into the air as if in a boiling passion. 'How could anyone offer so pitiful a sum to a lady with such attractions and accomplishments?'

"'My accomplishments, sir, may be less than you imagine,' said I. 'A little French, a little German, music and drawing—'

"'Tut-tut!' he cried. 'This is quite beside the question. Have you or have you not the bearing and deportment of a lady? If you have not, you are not fitted for the rearing of a child who may someday play a considerable part in the history of the country. But if you have, how could any gentleman ask you to accept anything under three figures? Your salary with me, madam, would commence at a hundred pounds a year.'

"You may imagine, Mr. Holmes, that such an offer seemed almost too good to be true, for the little money I had saved was beginning to run short. The gentleman, seeing perhaps my look of incredulity, opened a pocketbook and took out a note. 'It is also my custom,' said he, smiling until his eyes were just two shining slits amid the creases of his face, 'to advance to my young ladies half their salary beforehand, so that they may meet any little expenses of their journey and their wardrobe.'

"It seemed to me that I had never met so thoughtful a man; yet there was something unnatural about the whole transaction which made me wish to know a little more before I committed myself.

"'May I ask where you live, sir?' said I.

"'Hampshire. Charming rural place. The Copper Beeches, five miles on the far side of Winchester. It is the most lovely country, my dear young lady, and the dearest old country house.'

"'And my duties, sir?'

"'One child—one dear little romper just six years old. Oh, if you could see him killing cockroaches with a slipper! Smack! Smack! Smack! Three gone before you would wink!' He leaned back in his chair and laughed his eyes into his head again.

"I was a little startled at the nature of the child's amusement, but the father's laughter made me think that perhaps he was joking. 'My sole duty, then,' I asked, 'is to take charge of a single child?'

"'No, no, not the sole, my dear young lady,' he cried. 'Your duty would be to obey any little commands which my wife might give, provided always that they were such commands as a lady might with propriety obey. In dress now, for example! We are faddy people, you know—faddy, but kindhearted. If you were asked to wear any dress which we might give you, you would not object, heh?'

"'No,' said I, considerably astonished at his words.

"'Or to cut your hair quite short before you come to us?'

"I could hardly believe my ears. As you may observe, Mr. Holmes, my hair is somewhat luxuriant, and of a rather peculiar tint of chestnut. It has been considered artistic. I could not dream of sacrificing it in this offhand fashion. 'I am afraid that is quite impossible,' said I.

"I could see a shadow pass over his face as I spoke. 'Ah, very well, then,' he said. 'It is a pity, because in other respects you would have done very nicely. In that case, Miss Stoper, I had best inspect a few more of your young ladies.'

"The manageress glanced at me with much annoyance upon her face. 'Then good day to you, Miss Hunter,' she said sharply. She struck a gong upon the table, and I was shown out by the page.

"Well, Mr. Holmes, when I got back to my lodgings and found little enough in the cupboard, and two or three bills upon the table, I began to ask myself whether I had not done a very foolish thing. After all, if these people had strange fads, and expected obedience on the most extraordinary matters, they were at least ready to pay for their eccentricity. Besides, what use was my hair to me? Many people are improved by wearing it short, and perhaps I should be among the number. Next day I was inclined to think that I had made a mistake. By the day after I was almost ready to overcome my pride and go back to the agency to inquire whether the place was still open, when I received this letter. I will read it to you:

"The Copper Beeches, near Winchester

Dear Miss Hunter,

Miss Stoper has very kindly given me your address, and I write to ask you whether you have reconsidered your decision. My wife is very anxious that you should come, for she has been much attracted by my description of you. We are willing to give you one hundred twenty pounds a year, so as to recompense you for any little inconvenience which our fads may cause you. They are not very exacting after all. My wife is fond of a particular shade of electric blue, and would like you to wear such a dress indoors in the morning. You need not, however, go to the expense of purchasing one as we have one belonging to my dear daughter Alice (now in Philadelphia) which should fit you very well. Then, as to sitting here or there, that need cause you no inconvenience. As regards your hair, it is a pity, especially as I could not help remarking its beauty during our short interview, but I must remain firm upon this point, and I only hope that the increased salary may recompense you for the loss. Your duties, as far as the child is concerned, are very light. Now do try to come, and I shall meet you with the dogcart at Winchester. Let me know your train.

Yours faithfully,
Jephro Rucastle

"My mind is made up that I will accept, Mr. Holmes. I thought, however, that before taking the final step, I should like to submit the matter to your consideration. What is the meaning of it all?"

"Ah, I have no data. I cannot tell. Perhaps you have yourself formed some opinion?"

"Well, Mr. Rucastle seemed to be a kind, good-natured man. Is it not possible that his wife is a lunatic, that he desires to keep the matter quiet for fear she should be taken to an asylum, and that he humors her fancies in order to prevent an outbreak?"

"That is a possible solution—in fact, as matters stand, it is the most probable one. But I confess that it is not a situation which I should like to see a sister of mine apply for."

"But the money, Mr. Holmes, the money!"

"Well, yes, of course, the pay is good—too good. That is what makes me uneasy. Why should they give you one hundred twenty pounds a year, when they could have their pick for forty pounds?"

"I thought that if I told you the circumstances you would understand afterwards if I wanted your help. I should feel so much stronger if I felt that you were at the back of me."

"Oh, you may carry that feeling away with you. Your little problem promises to be the most interesting which has come my way for some months. There is something distinctly novel about some of the features. If you should find yourself in danger—"

"Danger! What danger do you foresee?"

Holmes shook his head gravely. "It would cease to be a danger if we could define it," said he. "But at any time, day or night, a telegram would bring me down to your help."

"That is enough." She rose briskly with the anxiety all swept from her face. "I shall write to Mr. Rucastle at once, sacrifice my poor hair tonight, and start for Winchester tomorrow, quite easy in my mind." With a few grateful words to Holmes she bade us good night, and bustled off upon her way.

"At least," said I, as we heard her quick, firm step descending the stairs, "she seems to be a young lady who is very well able to take care of herself."

"And she would need to be," said Holmes gravely. "I am much mistaken if we do not hear from her before many days are past."

The telegram which we eventually received came a fortnight later, just as I was thinking of turning in, and Holmes was settling down to one of those all-night researches which he frequently indulged in, when I would leave him stooping over a retort and a test tube, and find him in the same position when I came down to breakfast in the morning. He opened the yellow envelope, and then, glancing at the message, threw it across to me.

The summons was brief and urgent:

PLEASE BE AT THE BLACK SWAN AT WINCHESTER AT MIDDAY TO-MORROW. I AM AT MY WITS' END. HUNTER.

"Will you come with me?" asked Holmes, glancing up.

"I should wish to."

"Just look up the trains in *Bradshaw*, then."

"There is a train at half past nine," said I, glancing over the schedule. "It is due at Winchester at eleven thirty."

"That will do. Then I had better postpone my analysis of the acetones, as we may need to be at our best in the morning."

By eleven o'clock the next day we were well upon our way to the old English capital. It was an ideal spring day, a light blue sky, flecked with little fleecy white clouds drifting across from west to east. The sun was shining brightly, and yet there was an exhilarating nip in the air. All over the countryside, away to the rolling hills around Aldershot, the little red and gray roofs of the farmsteadings peeped out from amidst the light green of the new foliage.

"Are they not fresh and beautiful?" I cried, with all the enthusiasm of a man fresh from the fogs of Baker Street.

But Holmes shook his head gravely. "Do you know, Watson," said he, "that it is one of the curses of a mind like mine that I must look at everything with reference to my own special subject. You look at these scattered houses, and you are impressed by their beauty. I look at them with a feeling of their isolation, and of the impunity with which crime may be committed there. It is my belief, founded upon my experience, that the lowest alleys in London do not present a more dreadful record of sin than does the smiling and beautiful countryside."

"You horrify me!"

"But the reason is obvious. Look at these lonely houses, each in its own field, filled for the most part with poor ignorant folk who know little of the law. Think of the deeds of hellish cruelty which may go on in such places, and none the wiser. Had this lady who appeals to us for help gone to live in Winchester, I should never have had a fear for her. It is the five miles of country which makes the danger. Still, it is clear that she is not personally threatened."

"No. If she can meet us in Winchester she is free to get away."

"Quite so. Well, there is the tower of the Cathedral, and we shall soon learn all that Miss Hunter has to tell."

The Black Swan is an inn of repute in the High Street, and there we found the young lady waiting for us. She had engaged a sitting room, and our lunch awaited us upon the table.

"I am so delighted that you have come," she said earnestly. "Indeed, I do not know what I should do. Your advice will be altogether invaluable to me."

"Pray tell us what has happened to you."

"I will do so, and I must be quick, for I have promised Mr. Rucastle to be back before three. I got his leave to come into town this morning, though he little knew for what purpose."

"Let us have everything in its due order." Holmes thrust his long thin legs out towards the fire, and composed himself to listen.

"In the first place, it is only fair to say that I have met with no actual ill-treatment from Mr. and Mrs. Rucastle. But I am not easy in my mind about them. When I came down Mr. Rucastle met me here, and drove me in his dogcart to the Copper Beeches. It is, as he said, beautifully situated, but it is not beautiful in itself, for it is a large square block of a house, whitewashed, but all stained and streaked with damp and bad weather. There are grounds round it, woods on three sides, and on the fourth a field which slopes down to the Southampton highroad, which curves past about a hundred yards from the front door. A clump of copper beeches immediately in front of the hall door has given its name to the place.

"I was driven over by my employer, who was as amiable as ever, and was introduced by him to his wife and child. Mrs. Rucastle, I found, is not mad. She is a silent, pale-faced woman, much younger than her husband. From their conversation I have gathered that they have been married about seven years, that he was a widower, and that his only child by the first wife was the daughter who has gone to Philadelphia. Mr. Rucastle told me in private that she had left them because she had an unreasoning aversion to her step-mother. As the daughter could not have been less than twenty, I can quite imagine that her position must have been uncomfortable with her father's young wife.

"It was easy to see that Mrs. Rucastle was passionately devoted both to her husband and to her little son. Her eyes wandered continually from one to the other, noting every little want and forestalling it if possible. Mr. Rucastle was kind to her also in his bluff, boisterous fashion; and yet she had some secret sorrow, this woman. She would often be lost in deep thought, with the saddest look upon her face. I have thought sometimes that it was the disposition of her child which weighed upon her mind, for I have never met so utterly spoilt and so ill-natured a little creature. His whole life appears to be spent in an alternation between savage fits of passion and gloomy intervals of sulking. Giving pain to any creature weaker than himself seems to be his one idea of amusement, and he shows quite remarkable talent in planning the capture of mice, little birds, and insects. But I would rather not talk about him, Mr. Holmes, and, indeed, he has little to do with my story."

"I am glad of all details," remarked my friend, "whether they seem to you to be relevant or not."

"I shall try not to miss anything of importance. I was struck at once by the appearance and conduct of the servants. There are only two, a man and his wife. Toller, for that's his name, is a rough, uncouth man, with grizzled hair and whiskers, and a perpetual smell of drink. Twice since I have been with them he has been quite drunk. His wife is a very tall and strong woman with a sour face, as silent as Mrs. Rucastle, and much less amiable.

"For two days after my arrival at the Copper Beeches my life was very quiet; on the third, Mrs. Rucastle came down just after breakfast and whispered something to her husband. 'Oh, yes,' said he, turning to me, 'we are very much obliged to you, Miss Hunter, for falling in with our whims so far as to cut your hair. We shall now see how the electric-blue dress will become you. You will find it laid out upon the bed in your room, and if you would be so good as to put it on we should both be extremely obliged.'

"The dress which I found waiting for me was of a peculiar shade of blue. It was of excellent material, but it bore unmistakable signs of having been worn before. It would not have been a better fit if I had been measured for it. Both Mr. and Mrs. Rucastle expressed a delight at the look of it which seemed quite exaggerated in its vehemence. They were waiting for me in the drawing room, which is a very large room stretching along the entire front of the house, with three long windows reaching down to the floor. A chair had been placed close to the central window, with its back turned towards it. In this I was asked to sit, and then Mr. Rucastle, walking up and down on the other side of the room, began to tell me a series of the funniest stories that I have ever listened to. I laughed until I was quite weary. Mrs. Rucastle, however, who has evidently no sense of humor, sat with her hands in her lap, and an anxious look upon her face. After an hour or so, Mr. Rucastle suddenly remarked that I might change my dress, and go to little Edward in the nursery.

"Two days later this same performance was gone through under exactly similar circumstances. Again I changed my dress, again I sat in the window, and again I laughed very heartily at the funny stories of which my employer had an immense repertoire. Then he handed me a yellow-backed novel, and, moving my chair a little sideways, that my own shadow might not fall upon the page, he begged me to read aloud to him. I read for about ten minutes, and then suddenly, in the middle of a sentence, he ordered me to cease and change my dress.

"You can easily imagine, Mr. Holmes, how curious I became as to the meaning of this extraordinary performance. They were always very careful to turn my face away from the window, so that I became consumed with the desire to see what was going on behind my back. At first it seemed to be impossible, but I soon devised a means. My hand mirror had been broken, so I concealed a little of the glass in my handkerchief. On the next occasion, in the midst of my laughter, I put my handkerchief up to my eyes, and was able with a little management to see all that was behind me. There was a small bearded man in a gray suit standing in the Southampton road, leaning against the railings which bordered our field, and looking earnestly in my direction. I lowered my handkerchief, and glanced at Mrs. Rucastle to find her eyes fixed upon me with a most searching gaze. I am convinced that she had divined that I had a mirror in my hand, and had seen what was behind me.

"She rose at once. 'Jephro,' said she, 'there is a fellow upon the road there who stares up at Miss Hunter.'

" 'No friend of yours, Miss Hunter?' he asked.

" 'No. I know no one in these parts.'

" 'Dear me! How very impertinent! Kindly turn round, and motion him to go away.'

"I did as I was told, and at the same instant Mrs. Rucastle drew down the blind. That was a week ago, and from that time I have not sat again in the window, nor have I worn the blue dress, nor seen the man in the road."

"Pray continue," said Holmes. "Your narrative promises to be a most interesting one."

"You will find it rather disconnected, I fear. On the very first day that I was at Copper Beeches, Mr. Rucastle took me to a small out-building which stands near the kitchen door.

"'Look in here!' said he, showing me a slit between two planks. 'Is he not a beauty?'

"I looked through, and was conscious of two glowing eyes, and of a vague figure huddled up in the darkness.

"'Don't be frightened,' said my employer, laughing at the start which I had given. 'It's only Carlo, my mastiff. I call him mine, but really old Toller, my groom, is the only man who can do anything with him. We feed him once a day, and not too much then, so that he is always as keen as mustard. Toller lets him loose every night, and God help the trespasser he lays his fangs upon. Don't you ever on any pretext set your foot over the threshold at night, for it is as much as your life is worth.'

"The warning was no idle one, for two nights later I happened to look out of my bedroom window about two o'clock in the morning. It was a beautiful moonlight night, and the lawn in front of the house was silvered over and almost as bright as day. I was standing rapt in the peaceful beauty of the scene, when I was aware that something was moving under the shadow of the copper beeches. As it emerged into the moonshine I saw what it was. It was a giant dog, as large as a calf, tawny-tinted, with hanging jowl, black muzzle, and huge projecting bones. It walked slowly across the lawn and vanished into the shadow upon the other side. That dreadful silent sentinel sent a chill to my heart.

"And now I have a very strange experience to tell you. I had, as you know, cut off my hair in London, and I had placed it in a great coil at the bottom of my trunk. One evening, after the child was in bed, I began to rearrange my things. There was a chest of drawers in my room, the two upper ones empty and open, the lower one locked. I had filled the two first with my linen, and as I had still much to pack away, I was annoyed at not having the use of the third drawer. It struck me that it might have been fastened by a mere oversight, so I took out my bunch of keys and tried to open it. The very first key fitted, and I drew the drawer open. There was only one thing in it, but I am sure that you would never guess what it was.

"It was my coil of hair. I took it up and examined it. It was of the same peculiar tint, and the same thickness. But then how *could* my hair have been locked in the drawer? With trembling hands I undid my trunk, and drew from the bottom my own hair. I laid the two tresses together, and they were identical. Puzzle as I would, I could make nothing at all of what it meant. I returned the strange hair to the drawer, and I said nothing of the matter to the Rucastles, as I felt that I had put myself in the wrong by opening a drawer which they had locked.

"I am naturally observant, as you may have remarked, Mr. Holmes, and I soon had a plan of the whole house in my head. There was one wing which appeared not to be inhabited. A door which faced that which led into the quarters of the Tollers opened into this suite, but it was invariably locked.

"One day I met Mr. Rucastle coming out through this door, his keys in his hand. His cheeks were red, his brow was all crinkled with anger, and the veins stood out at his temple with passion. He locked the door, and hurried past me without a word.

"This aroused my curiosity; so when I went out for a walk in the grounds with my charge, I strolled round to the side from which I could see the windows of this part of the house. There were three of them in a row, two of which were simply dirty, while the third was shuttered up. As I strolled up and down, glancing at them occasionally, Mr. Rucastle came out to me.

"'Ah!' said he, looking his jovial self again. 'You must not think me rude if I passed you without a word, my dear young lady. I was preoccupied with business matters.'

"I assured him that I was not offended. 'By the way,' said I, 'you seem to have quite a suite of spare rooms up there, and one of them has the shutters up.'

"'Photography is one of my hobbies,' said he. 'I have made my darkroom up there. But, dear me, what an observant young lady we have come upon. Who would have believed it?' He spoke in a jesting tone, but there was no jest in his eyes.

"Well, Mr. Holmes, from the moment that I understood that there was something about that suite of rooms which I was not to know, I was all on fire to go over them. It was not mere curiosity. It was more a feeling that some good might come from my penetrating to this place. They talk of woman's instinct; perhaps it was woman's instinct which gave me that feeling. At any rate, I was keenly on the lookout for any chance to pass the forbidden door.

"It was only yesterday that the chance came. I may tell you that, besides Mr. Rucastle, both Toller and his wife find something to do in these deserted rooms. Yesterday evening Toller was very drunk; and, when I came upstairs, there was the key in the door. I have no doubt that he had left it there. Mr. and Mrs. Rucastle were both downstairs, with the child, so that I had an admirable opportunity. I turned the key gently in the lock, opened the door, and slipped through.

"There was a little passage in front of me, unpapered and uncarpeted, which turned at a right angle at the farther end. Round this corner were three doors in a line, the first and third of which were open. They each led into an empty room, dusty and cheerless, their windows so thick with dirt that the evening light glimmered dimly through them. The center door was closed, and across the outside of it had been fastened one of the broad bars of an iron bed, padlocked at one end to a ring in the wall, and fastened at the other with stout cord. The door itself was locked, and the key was not there. This barricaded door corresponded clearly with the shuttered window outside, and yet I could see by the glimmer from beneath it that the room was not in darkness. Evidently there was a skylight which let in light from above. As I stood in the passage, wondering what secret this sinister door might veil, I heard the sound of steps within the room, and saw a shadow pass across the slit of dim light which shone out from under the door. A mad, unreasoning terror rose up in me at the sight, Mr. Holmes, and I turned and ran—ran as though some dreadful hand were behind me, clutching at the skirt of my dress. I rushed down the passage, through the door, and straight into the arms of Mr. Rucastle, who was waiting outside.

"'So,' said he, smiling, 'it was you, then. I thought it must be when I saw the door open.'

"'Oh, I am so frightened!' I panted.

"'My dear young lady'—you cannot think how caressing and soothing his manner was—'and what has frightened you?'

"'I was foolish enough to go into the empty wing,' I answered. 'But it is so lonely and eerie in this dim light that I was frightened and ran out again. Oh, it is so dreadfully still in there!'

"'Only that?' said he, looking at me keenly, and still smiling in the most amiable manner.

"'Why, what do you think?' I asked.

"'Why do you think that I lock this door?'

"'I am sure I do not know.'

"'It is to keep people out who have no business there. And if you ever put your foot over that threshold again'—here in an instant his smile hardened into a grin of rage, and he glared down at me with the face of a demon—'I'll throw you to the mastiff.'

"I was so terrified that I do not know what I did, but I must have rushed past him into my room. I remember nothing until I found myself lying on my bed trembling all over. Then I thought of you, Mr. Holmes. I could not live there longer without some advice. I was frightened of the house, of the man, of the woman, of the servants, even of the child. Of course I might have fled from the house, but my curiosity was almost as strong as my fears. I put on my hat and cloak, went down to the office, which is about half a mile from the house, sent you a wire, and then returned, feeling very much easier. I slipped back in safety, and lay awake half the night in my joy at the thought of seeing you.

"I had no difficulty in getting leave to come into Winchester this morning, but I must be back before three o'clock, for Mr. and Mrs. Rucastle are going on a visit, and will be away all evening, so that I must look after the child. Now, Mr. Holmes, I should be very glad if you could tell me what it all means, and what I should do."

Holmes and I had listened spellbound to this extraordinary story. My friend rose now, and paced up and down, his hands in his pockets, and an expression of the most profound gravity upon his face. "Is Toller still drunk?" he asked.

"Yes. I heard his wife tell Mrs. Rucastle that she could do nothing with him."

"Is there a cellar with a good strong lock?"

"Yes, the wine cellar."

"You seem to me to have acted all through this matter like a brave and sensible girl, Miss Hunter. Do you think that you could perform one more feat? I should not ask it of you if I did not think you a quite exceptional woman."

"I will try. What is it?"

"We shall be at the Copper Beeches by seven o'clock, my friend and I. The Rucastles will be gone by that time, and Toller will, we hope, still be incapable. If you could send Mrs. Toller into the cellar, on some errand, and then turn the key upon her, you would facilitate matters immensely."

"I will do it."

"Excellent! We shall then look thoroughly into the affair. Of course there is only one feasible explanation. You have been brought there to personate someone, and the real person is imprisoned in this chamber. I have no doubt that this prisoner is the daughter, Miss Alice Rucastle, who was said to have gone to America. You were chosen, doubtless, as resembling her in height, figure, and the color of your hair. Hers had been cut off, possibly in some illness through which she has passed, and so yours had to be sacrificed also. By a curious chance you came upon her tresses. The man in the road was, undoubtedly, some friend of hers—possibly her fiancé—and no doubt as you wore the girl's dress, and were so like her, he was convinced from your laughter, whenever he saw you, and afterwards from your gesture, that Miss Rucastle was perfectly happy, and that she no longer desired his attentions. The dog is let loose at night to prevent him from communicating with her. So much is fairly clear. The most serious point in the case is the disposition of the child."

"What on earth has that to do with it?" I ejaculated.

"My dear Watson, you as a medical man are continually gaining light as to the tendencies of a child by the study of the parents. Don't you see that the converse is equally valid? I have frequently gained my first real insight into the character of parents by studying their children. This child's disposition is abnormally cruel, merely for cruelty's sake, and whether he derives this from his smiling father, as I should suspect, or from his mother, it bodes evil for the poor girl who is in their power."

"I am sure you are right," cried our client. "A thousand things come back to me which make me certain you have hit it. Oh, let us lose not an instant in bringing help to this poor creature."

"We must be circumspect, for we are dealing with a very cunning man. We can do nothing until seven o'clock. At that hour we shall be with you."

IT WAS JUST SEVEN when we reached the Copper Beeches, having put up our trap at a wayside public house. The group of trees, with their dark leaves shining like burnished metal in the light of the setting sun, were sufficient to mark the house even had Miss Hunter not been standing smiling on the doorstep.

"Have you managed it?" asked Holmes.

A loud thudding noise came from somewhere downstairs. "That is Mrs. Toller in the cellar," said she. "Her husband lies snoring on the kitchen rug. Here are his keys."

"You have done well!" cried Holmes with enthusiasm. "Now lead the way, and we shall soon see the end of this black business."

We passed up the stair, unlocked the door, followed on down a passage, and found ourselves in front of the barricade. Holmes cut the cord and dropped the transverse bar. Then he tried the various keys in the lock, but without success. No sound came from within, and at the silence Holmes's face clouded over.

"I trust that we are not too late," said he. "I think, Miss Hunter, that we had better go in without you. Now, Watson, put your shoulder to it, and we shall see whether we can make our way in."

It was an old rickety door and gave at once before our united strength. Together we rushed into the room. It was empty. There was no furniture save a pallet bed, a small table, and a basketful of linen. The skylight was open, and the prisoner gone. "There has been some villainy here," said Holmes. "This beauty has guessed Miss Hunter's intentions, and has carried his victim off."

"But how?"

"Through the skylight. We shall soon see how he managed it." He swung himself up onto the roof. "Ah, yes," he cried, "here's the end of a long light ladder against the eaves."

"But it is impossible," said Miss Hunter. "The ladder was not there when the Rucastles went away."

"He has come back and done it. I tell you that he is a clever and dangerous man. I should not be very much surprised if this were he whose step I hear now upon the stair. I think, Watson, that it would be well for you to have your pistol ready."

The words were hardly out of his mouth before a man appeared at the door of the room, a very fat and burly man, with a heavy stick in his hand. Miss Hunter screamed and shrank against the wall, but Holmes sprang forward and confronted him.

"You villain," said he, "where's your daughter?"

The fat man cast his eyes round, and then up at the open skylight. "It is for me to ask you that," he shrieked, "you thieves! Spies and thieves! I have caught you, have I? I'll serve you!" He turned and clattered down the stairs as hard as he could go.

"He's gone for the dog!" cried Miss Hunter.

"I have my revolver," said I.

We all rushed down the stairs together. We had hardly reached the front hall when we heard the baying of a hound, and then a scream of agony, with a horrible worrying sound. An elderly man with a red face and shaking limbs came staggering out at a side door.

"My God!" he cried. "Someone has loosed the dog. It's not been fed for two days. Quick, quick, or it'll be too late!"

Holmes and I rushed out, and round the angle of the house,

with Toller, who was now sober, hurrying behind us. There was the huge famished brute, its black muzzle buried in Rucastle's throat. Running up, I blew its brains out, and it fell over with its keen white teeth still meeting in the great creases of his neck. With much labor we separated them, and carried him, living but horribly mangled, into the house. We laid him upon the drawing-room sofa, and I did what I could to relieve his pain. We were all assembled round him when a tall, gaunt woman entered the room.

"Mrs. Toller!" cried Miss Hunter.

"Yes, miss. Mr. Rucastle let me out when he came back. Ah, miss, it is a pity you didn't let me know what you were planning, for I would have told you that your pains were wasted."

"Ha!" said Holmes, looking keenly at her. "It is clear that Mrs. Toller knows more about this matter than anyone else."

"Yes, sir, I do, and I am ready enough to tell what I know."

"Then pray sit down, and let us hear it, for there are several points on which I must confess that I am still in the dark."

"I will soon make it clear to you," said she; "and if there's police-court business over this, you'll remember that I was the one that stood your friend, and that I was Miss Alice's friend too.

"She was never happy at home, Miss Alice wasn't, from the time that her father married again. She was slighted like, and had no say in anything; but it never really became bad for her until after she met Mr. Fowler at a friend's house. As well as I could learn, Miss Alice had rights of her own by will, but she was so quiet and patient that she just left everything in Mr. Rucastle's hands. He knew he was safe with her; but when there was a chance of a husband coming forward, who would ask for all that the law could give him, then her father thought it time to put a stop on it. He wanted her to sign a paper so that, whether she married or not, he could use her money. When she wouldn't do it, he kept on worrying her until she got brain fever, and for six weeks was at death's door. Then she got better at last, all worn to a shadow, and with her beautiful hair cut off; but that didn't change her young man, and he stuck to her as true as could be."

"Ah," said Holmes, "I think that what you have been good

enough to tell us makes the matter fairly clear, and that I can deduce all that remains. Mr. Rucastle, then, I presume, took to this system of imprisonment, and brought Miss Hunter down from London in order to get rid of the disagreeable persistence of Mr. Fowler. But Mr. Fowler, being a persevering man, blockaded the house, and succeeded by certain arguments, metallic or otherwise, in convincing you that your interests were the same as his."

"Mr. Fowler was a very kind-spoken, freehanded gentleman," said Mrs. Toller serenely.

"And in this way he managed that your good man should have no want of drink, and that a ladder should be ready at the moment when your master had gone out."

"You have it, sir, just as it happened."

"I am sure we owe you an apology, Mrs. Toller," said Holmes, "for you have certainly cleared up everything which puzzled us. And here comes the country surgeon and Mrs. Rucastle, so I think, Watson, that we had best escort Miss Hunter back to Winchester."

AND THUS WAS SOLVED the mystery of the sinister house with the copper beeches in front of the door. Mr. Rucastle survived, but was always a broken man, kept alive solely through the care of his devoted wife. They still live with their old servants, who probably know so much of Rucastle's past life that he finds it difficult to part from them. Mr. Fowler and Miss Rucastle were married, by special license, in Southampton the day after their flight, and he is now the holder of a government appointment in the Island of Mauritius. As to Miss Violet Hunter, my friend Holmes, rather to my disappointment, manifested no further interest in her when once she had ceased to be the center of one of his problems, and she is now the head of a private school at Walsall, where I believe that she has met with considerable success.

HOLMES HAD BEEN SEATED for some hours in silence with his long, thin back curved over a chemical vessel in which he was brewing a particularly malodorous product. His head was sunk upon his breast, and he looked from my point of view like a strange, lank bird with dull gray plumage and a black topknot.

"So, Watson," said he suddenly, "you do not propose to invest in South African securities?"

I gave a start of astonishment. "How on earth do you know that?" I asked.

He wheeled round upon his stool, with a steaming test tube in his hand, and a gleam of amusement in his deep-set eyes. "You see, my dear Watson"—he propped his test tube in the rack, and began to lecture with the air of a professor addressing his class— "it was not really difficult, by an inspection of the groove between your left forefinger and thumb, to feel sure that you did *not* propose to invest your small capital in the goldfields."

"I see no connection."

"Very likely not; but here are the missing links of the very simple chain of inference: One. You had chalk between your left finger and thumb when you returned from the club last night. Two. You put chalk there when you play billiards, to steady the cue. Three. You never play billiards except with Thurston. Four. You told me, four weeks ago, that Thurston had an option on some South African property which would expire in a month, and which he desired you to share with him. Five. Your checkbook is locked in my drawer, and you have not asked for the key. Six. You do not propose to invest your money in this manner."

"How absurdly simple!" I cried.

"Quite so!" said he, a little nettled. "Every problem becomes very childish when once it is explained to you. Here is an un-explained one. See what you can make of it." He tossed me a sheet of paper, and turned once more to his chemical analysis.

I looked with amazement at the absurd hieroglyphics upon the paper. "Why, Holmes, it is a child's drawing," I cried.

"Oh, that's your idea!"

"What else should it be?"

"That is what Mr. Hilton Cubitt, of Riding Thorpe Manor, Norfolk, is very anxious to know. This little conundrum came by the first post, and he was to follow by the next train. There's a ring at the bell, Watson. I should not be very much surprised if this were he."

A heavy step was heard upon the stairs, and an instant later there entered a tall, clean-shaven gentleman with clear eyes and ruddy cheeks. He seemed to bring with him a whiff of strong, fresh, bracing, east-coast air. Having shaken hands with us, he was about to sit down, when his eye rested upon the paper with the curious markings. "Well, Mr. Holmes, what do you make of these?" he cried. "They told me you were fond of queer mysteries, and I don't think you can find a queerer one than that."

"At first sight it would appear to be some childish prank," said Holmes. "Why should you attribute any importance to it?"

"I never should, Mr. Holmes. But my wife does. It is frighten-ing her to death. That's why I want to clear up the matter."

Holmes held up the paper so that the sunlight shone full upon it. It was a page torn from a notebook. The markings were done in pencil, and ran in this way:

Holmes examined it for some time, and then, folding it carefully, he placed it in his pocketbook. "This promises to be a most in-teresting case," said he. "You gave me a few particulars in your letter, Mr. Hilton Cubitt, but I should be much obliged if you would go over it again for the benefit of my friend, Dr. Watson."

"I'll begin at the time of my marriage last year," said our visitor, nervously clasping and unclasping his great, strong hands. "But I want to say first of all that my people have been at Riding Thorpe for a matter of five centuries, and there is no better-known family in the County of Norfolk. Last year I came up to London on business, and I stopped at a boardinghouse in Russell Square. There was an American young lady there—Elsie Patrick was the name. In some way we became friends, until before my month was up I was as much in love as man could be. We were quietly married at a registry office, and we returned to Norfolk a wedded couple. You'll think it mad, Mr. Holmes, that a man of a good old family should marry a wife in this fashion, knowing nothing of her past or of her people, but if you saw her and knew her, it would help you to understand.

"I can't say that Elsie did not give me every chance of getting out of it if I wished to do so. 'I have had some very disagreeable associations in my life,' said she. 'I wish to forget all about them. I would rather never allude to the past, for it is very painful to me. If you take me, Hilton, you will take a woman who has nothing that she need be personally ashamed of; but you will have to be content with my word for it, and to allow me to be silent about the past. If these conditions are too hard, then go back to Norfolk, and leave me to the lonely life in which you found me.' I told her that I was content to take her on her own terms, and I have been as good as my word.

"Well, we have been married now for a year, and very happy we have been. But about a month ago I saw for the first time signs of trouble. One day my wife received a letter with an American stamp. She turned deadly white, read the letter, and threw it into the fire. She made no allusion to it afterwards, and I made none, but she has never known an easy hour from that moment. There is always a look of fear upon her face—a look as if she were waiting and expecting. She would do better to trust me. She would find that I was her best friend. But until she speaks, I can say nothing. Mind you, she is a truthful woman, Mr. Holmes, and whatever trouble there may have been in her past life it has been no fault of hers—of that I am sure.

"Well, about a week ago I found on one of the windowsills a number of absurd little dancing figures like these upon the paper. They were scrawled with chalk. I thought that it was the stable-boy who had drawn them, but the lad swore he knew nothing about it. Anyhow, they had come there during the night. I had them washed out, and I only mentioned the matter to my wife afterwards. To my surprise, she took it very seriously, and begged me if any more came to let her see them. None did come for a week, and then yesterday morning I found this paper lying on the sundial in the garden. I showed it to Elsie, and down she dropped in a dead faint. Since then she has looked half dazed, with terror always lurking in her eyes. It was then that I sent the paper to you, Mr. Holmes. It was not a thing that I could take to the police, for they would have laughed at me, but you will tell me what to do. I am not a rich man, but if there is any danger threatening my little woman, I would spend my last copper to shield her."

He was a fine creature, this man of the old English soil—simple, straight, and gentle, with his earnest blue eyes and broad, comely face. His love for his wife and his trust in her shone in his features. Holmes had listened to him with the utmost attention, and now he sat for some time in silent thought.

"Don't you think, Mr. Cubitt," said he, at last, "that your best plan would be to make a direct appeal to your wife, and to ask her to share her secret with you?"

Hilton Cubitt shook his massive head. "A promise is a promise, Mr. Holmes. If Elsie wished to tell me she would. If not, it is not for me to force her confidence. But I am justified in taking my own line—and I will."

"Then I will help you with all my heart. First, have you heard of any strangers being seen in your immediate neighborhood?"

"No. But we have several small watering places not far away. And the farmers take in lodgers."

"These hieroglyphics have evidently a meaning. If it is a purely arbitrary one, it may be impossible for us to solve it. If, on the other hand, it is systematic, I have no doubt that we shall get to the bottom of it. But this particular sample is so short and the facts which you have brought me are so indefinite that we have no basis for an investigation. I would suggest that you return to Norfolk, that you keep a keen lookout for strangers, and that you take an exact copy of any fresh dancing men which may appear. When you have collected some new evidence, come to me again. If there are any pressing developments, I shall be always ready to run down and see you in your Norfolk home."

The interview left Holmes very thoughtful, and several times in the next few days I saw him take the slip of paper from his notebook and look earnestly at the curious figures inscribed upon it. He made no allusion to the affair, however, until one afternoon a fortnight or so later. I was going out when he called me back. "You had better stay here, Watson."

"Why?"

"Because I had a wire from Hilton Cubitt this morning. He may be here at any moment. I gather that there have been some new incidents of importance."

We had not long to wait for our Norfolk squire. He arrived looking worried and depressed. "It's getting on my nerves, this business, Mr. Holmes," said he, as he sank into an armchair. "It's bad enough to feel that you are surrounded by unseen, unknown folk, who have some kind of design upon you, but when, in addition to that, you know that it is killing your wife by inches, then it becomes as much as flesh and blood can endure."

"Has she said anything yet?"

"No, Mr. Holmes. There have been times when the poor girl has spoken about my old family, and our unsullied honor, and I always felt it was leading to the point, but somehow it turned off before we got there. I have several fresh dancing-men pictures for you to examine, and, what is more important, I have seen the fellow."

"What, the man who draws them?"

"Yes, I saw him at his work. But I will tell you everything in order. When I got back after my visit to you, the very first thing I saw next morning was a fresh crop of dancing men. They had been drawn in chalk upon the black wooden door of the toolhouse, which stands beside the lawn in full view of the front windows. I took an exact copy, and here it is." He unfolded a paper and laid it upon the table. Here are the hieroglyphics:

"Excellent!" said Holmes. "Excellent! Pray continue."

"When I had taken the copy, I rubbed out the marks, but, two mornings later, a fresh inscription had appeared. Here it is:"

Holmes rubbed his hands and chuckled with delight.

"Three days later this message was left scrawled upon paper, and placed under a pebble upon the sundial. The characters are, as you see, exactly the same as the last ones. After that I determined to lie in wait, so I got out my revolver and I sat up in my study, which overlooks the lawn and garden. About two in the morning I was seated by the window, all being dark save for the moonlight outside, when I heard steps behind me, and there was my wife in her dressing gown. She implored me to come to bed. I told her frankly that I wished to see who it was who played such absurd tricks upon us. She answered that it was some senseless practical joke, and that I should not take any notice of it.

"Suddenly, as she spoke, I saw her white face grow whiter yet in the moonlight, and her hand tightened upon my shoulder. Something was moving in the shadow of the toolhouse. I saw a dark, creeping figure which crawled round the corner and squatted in front of the door. Seizing my pistol, I was rushing out, when my wife threw her arms round me and held me with convulsive strength. At last I got clear, but by the time I had opened the door and reached the toolhouse the creature was gone. There on the door, however, was the very same arrangement of dancing men which had already twice appeared, and which I have copied on that paper. There was no other sign of the fellow anywhere, though I ran all over the grounds. And yet when I examined the door again in the morning, he had scrawled some more of his pictures under the line which I had already seen. The fresh drawing was very short, but I made a copy of it, and here it is."

Again he produced a paper. The new dance was in this form:

"Tell me," said Holmes—and I could see by his eyes that he was much excited—"was this a mere addition to the first or did it appear to be entirely separate?"

"It was on a different panel of the door."

"Excellent! This is far the most important of all for our purpose. It fills me with hopes. Now, Mr. Hilton Cubitt, how long can you stay in London?"

"I must go back today. I would not leave my wife alone all night for anything."

"I daresay you are right. Leave me these papers, and I think that it is very likely that I shall be able to pay you a visit shortly and to throw some light upon your case."

The moment that Hilton Cubitt's broad back had disappeared through the door Sherlock Holmes rushed to the table, laid out all the slips of paper containing dancing men in front of him, and threw himself into an intricate and elaborate calculation. For two hours he covered sheet after sheet of paper with figures and letters. Sometimes he whistled and sang at his work; sometimes he was puzzled, and would sit for long spells with a furrowed brow and a vacant eye. Finally he sprang from his chair with a cry of satisfaction, and walked up and down the room rubbing his hands together. Then he wrote a long telegram upon a cable form. "If my answer to this is as I hope, it will be a very pretty case, Watson," said he. "I expect that we shall be able to go down to Norfolk tomorrow, and to take our friend some very definite news as to the secret of his annoyance."

I was filled with curiosity, but I was aware that Holmes liked to make his disclosures at his own time and in his own way, so I waited until it should suit him to take me into his confidence. But there was a delay in that answering telegram, and two days of impatience followed, during which Holmes pricked up his ears at every ring of the bell. On the evening of the second there came a letter from Hilton Cubitt. All was quiet with him, save that a long inscription had appeared that morning upon the pedestal of the sundial. He enclosed a copy of it:

Holmes bent over this grotesque frieze for some minutes, and then sprang to his feet with an exclamation of surprise and dismay. "We have let this affair go far enough," said he. "We shall breakfast early tomorrow morning and take the very first train to North Walsham. Ah! Here is our expected cablegram. One moment, Mrs. Hudson, there may be an answer. No, that is quite as I expected. This message makes it even more essential that we should let Hilton Cubitt know how matters stand, for it is a dangerous web in which our simple Norfolk squire is entangled."

So, indeed, it proved, and as I come to the dark conclusion of a story which had seemed to me to be only childish and bizarre, I experience once again the horror with which I was filled. Would that I had some brighter ending to communicate to my readers, but these are the chronicles of fact, and I must follow to their dark crisis the strange events which for some days made Riding Thorpe Manor a household word through the length and breadth of England.

WE HAD HARDLY ALIGHTED at North Walsham, and mentioned the name of our destination, when the stationmaster hurried towards us. "I suppose that you are the detectives from London?" said he.

A look of annoyance passed over Holmes's face. "What makes you think such a thing?"

"Because Inspector Martin from Norwich has just passed

through. But maybe you are the surgeons. You may be in time to save her yet—though it be for the gallows."

Holmes's brow was dark with anxiety. "We are going to Riding Thorpe Manor," said he, "but we have heard nothing of what has passed there."

"It's a terrible business," said the stationmaster. "They are shot, both Mr. Hilton Cubitt and his wife. She shot him and then herself—so the servants say. He's dead and her life is despaired of. Dear, dear, one of the oldest families in the County of Norfolk, and one of the most honored."

Holmes hurried to a carriage, and during the seven miles' drive he never opened his mouth. Seldom have I seen him so despondent. He leaned back in his seat, lost in gloomy speculation, until at last the violet rim of the German Ocean appeared over the edge of the Norfolk coast, and the driver pointed with his whip to two old brick and timber gables which projected from a grove of trees. "That's Riding Thorpe Manor," said he.

As we drove up to the porticoed front door, I observed near it the black toolhouse and the pedestaled sundial with which we had such strange associations. A dapper little man, with a quick, alert manner and a waxed mustache, had just descended from a high dogcart. He introduced himself as Inspector Martin, of the Norfolk Constabulary, and he was considerably astonished when he heard the name of my companion.

"Why, Mr. Holmes, the crime was only committed at three this morning. How could you hear of it in London and get to the spot so soon?"

"I anticipated it. I came in the hope of preventing it."

"Then you must have evidence of which we are ignorant, for they were said to be a most united couple," said the inspector.

"I have only the evidence of the dancing men," said Holmes. "I will explain the matter to you later. Meanwhile, since it is too late to prevent this tragedy, I am very anxious that I should use the knowledge which I possess in order to ensure that justice be done. Will you associate me in your investigation, or will you prefer that I should act independently?"

"I should be proud to feel we were acting together, Mr. Holmes," said the inspector earnestly.

"In that case I should be glad to hear the evidence and to examine the premises without an instant of unnecessary delay."

Inspector Martin had the good sense to allow my friend to do things in his own fashion, and contented himself with carefully noting the results. The local surgeon, an old, white-haired man, had just come down from Mrs. Hilton Cubitt's room, and he reported that her injuries were serious, but not necessarily fatal. The bullet had passed through the front of her brain, and it would probably be some time before she could regain consciousness. The bullet had been discharged at very close quarters. There was only the one pistol found in the room, two barrels of which had been emptied. Mr. Hilton Cubitt had been shot through the heart. It was equally conceivable that he had shot her and then himself, or that she had been the criminal, for the revolver lay upon the floor midway between them.

"Has he been moved?" asked Holmes.

"We have moved nothing except the lady. We could not leave her lying wounded upon the floor."

"Is anyone else here?"

"Yes, the constable. The housemaid, Saunders, and Mrs. King, the cook, are in the kitchen."

"Then I think we had better hear their story at once."

The old hall, oak-paneled and high-windowed, was turned into a court of investigation. Holmes sat in a great, old-fashioned chair, his inexorable eyes gleaming out of his haggard face. I could read in them a set purpose to avenge the client he had failed to save. Inspector Martin, the country doctor, myself, and a stolid village policeman made up the rest of that strange company.

The two women told their story clearly enough. They had been aroused from their sleep by the sound of an explosion, which had been followed a minute later by a second one. They slept in adjoining rooms, and Mrs. King had rushed in to Saunders. Together they had descended the stairs. The door of the study was open, and a candle was burning upon the table. Their master lay upon his face in the center of the room. He was quite dead. Near the window his wife was crouching, her head leaning against the wall, her face red with blood. She breathed heavily, but was incapable of saying anything. The passage, as well as the room, was full of smoke and the smell of powder. The window was shut and fastened upon the inside. Both women were positive upon the point. They had at once sent for the doctor and for the constable. Then, with the aid of the groom and the stableboy, they had conveyed their injured mistress to her room. Both she and her husband had occupied the bed. She was clad in her dress—he in his dressing gown, over his nightclothes. Nothing had been moved in the study. So far as they knew, there had never been any quarrel between husband and wife.

In answer to Inspector Martin, the servants were clear that every door was fastened upon the inside, and that no one could have escaped from the house. In answer to Holmes, they both remembered that they smelled powder from the moment that they ran out of their rooms upon the top floor. "I commend that fact to your attention," said Holmes to his professional colleague. "And now I think that we can undertake a thorough examination of the room."

The study proved to be a small chamber, lined on three sides with books, and with a writing table facing an ordinary window, which looked out upon the garden. Our first attention was given to the body of the unfortunate squire, whose huge frame lay stretched across the room. His disordered dress showed that he had been hastily aroused from sleep. The bullet had been fired at him from the front, and had remained in his body, after penetrating the heart. His death had certainly been instantaneous and painless. There was no powder marking either upon his dressing gown or on his hands. According to the country surgeon, the lady had stains upon her face, but none upon her hand.

"The absence of the latter means nothing, though its presence may mean everything," said Holmes. "Unless the powder from a badly fitting cartridge happens to spurt backward, one may fire many shots without leaving a sign. I would suggest that Mr.

Cubitt's body may now be removed. I suppose, Doctor, you have not recovered the bullet which wounded the lady?"

"A serious operation will be necessary before that can be done. But there are still four cartridges in the revolver. Two have been fired and two wounds inflicted, so that each bullet can be accounted for."

"So it would seem," said Holmes. "Perhaps you can account also for the bullet which has so obviously struck the edge of the window?" He had turned suddenly, and his long, thin finger was pointing to a hole which had been drilled right through the lower window sash, about an inch above the bottom.

"By George!" cried the inspector. "How ever did you see that?"

"Because I looked for it."

"Wonderful!" said the doctor. "You are certainly right, sir. Then a third shot has been fired, and therefore a third person must have been present. But who could that have been?"

"That is the problem which we are now about to solve," said Holmes. "You remember, Inspector Martin, when the servants said that on leaving their room they were at once conscious of a smell of powder, I remarked that the point was an extremely important one?"

"Yes, sir; but I confess I did not quite follow you."

"It suggested that at the time of the firing, the window as well as the door of the room had been open. Otherwise the fumes of powder could not have been blown so rapidly through the house. A draft in the room was necessary for that. Both door and window were only open for a very short time, however."

"How do you prove that?"

"Because the candle was not guttered."

"Capital!" cried the inspector. "Capital!"

"Feeling sure that the window had been open at the time of the tragedy, I conceived that there might have been a third person in the affair, who stood outside this opening and fired through it. Any shot directed at this person might hit the sash. I looked, and there, sure enough, was the bullet mark!"

"But how came the window to be shut and fastened?"

"The woman's first instinct would be to shut and fasten the window. But, halloa! What is this?"

It was a lady's handbag which stood upon the study table— a trim little bag of crocodile skin and silver. Holmes turned the contents out. There were twenty fifty-pound notes, held together by an india-rubber band—nothing else.

"This must be preserved, for it will figure in the trial," said Holmes, as he handed the bag with its contents to the inspector. "It is now necessary that we should try to throw some light upon this third bullet, which has clearly, from the splintering of the wood, been fired from inside the room. I should like to see Mrs. King, the cook, again." She was brought in and he questioned her further. "You said, Mrs. King, that you were awakened by an explosion that was shortly followed by a second one. You don't think it might have been two shots fired almost at the same instant?"

"I am sure I couldn't say, sir."

"I believe that it was undoubtedly so. Now, if you will kindly step round with me, Inspector Martin, we shall see what evidence the garden has to offer."

A flower bed extended up to the study window, and we all broke into an exclamation as we approached it. The flowers were trampled down, and the soft soil was imprinted all over with footmarks. Holmes hunted among the grass and leaves like a retriever after a wounded bird. Then, with a cry of satisfaction, he bent forward and picked up a little brazen cylinder. "I thought so," said he. "The revolver had an ejector, and here is the third cartridge. I think, Inspector, that our case is almost complete. Even if this lady should never recover consciousness, we can still reconstruct the events of last night, and ensure that justice be done. First of all, I wish to know whether there is any inn in this neighborhood known as Elrige's?"

The servants were cross-questioned, but none of them had heard of such a place. The stableboy remembered that a farmer of that name lived some miles off, in the direction of East Ruston.

"Is it a lonely farm?"

"Very lonely, sir."

"Perhaps they have not heard yet of what has happened here?"

"Maybe not, sir."

Holmes thought for a little, and then a curious smile played over his face. "Saddle a horse, my lad," said he. "I wish you to take a note to Elrige's Farm."

He took from his pocket the various slips of the dancing men. With these in front of him, he worked for some time at the study table. Finally he handed a note to the boy, with directions to put it into the hands of the person to whom it was addressed, and to answer no questions of any sort which might be put to him. I saw the outside of the note, addressed in straggling, irregular characters, very unlike Holmes's usual precise hand. It was consigned to Mr. Abe Slaney, Elrige's Farm, East Ruston, Norfolk.

"I think, Inspector," Holmes remarked, "that you would do well to telegraph for an escort, as, if my calculations prove to be correct, you may have a particularly dangerous prisoner to convey to the county jail. The boy who takes this note could no doubt forward your telegram. If there is an afternoon train to town, Watson, I think we should do well to take it, as I have a chemical analysis of some interest to finish, and this investigation draws rapidly to a close."

When the youth had been dispatched with the note, Holmes gave his instructions to the servants. If any visitor were to call asking for Mrs. Hilton Cubitt, no information should be given as to her condition, but he was to be shown at once into the drawing room. Then he led the way into the drawing room, with the remark that the business was now out of our hands, and that we must while away the time as best we might until we could see what was in store for us. The doctor departed to his patients, and only the inspector and myself remained.

"I think that I can help you to pass an hour in an interesting and profitable manner," said Holmes, drawing his chair up to the table, and spreading out in front of him the various papers upon which were recorded the antics of the dancing men. "I am fairly familiar with all forms of secret writings, and am myself the author of a trifling monograph upon the subject, but I confess that these singular productions are entirely new to me. The object of those who invented the system has apparently been to give the idea that they are the mere random sketches of children.

"Having once recognized, however, that the symbols stood for letters, and having applied the rules which guide us in all forms of secret writings, the solution was easy enough. The first message submitted to me was so short that it was impossible for me to do more than to say, with some confidence, that the symbol χ stood for E. As you are aware, E is the most common letter in the English alphabet, and even in a short sentence one would expect to find it most often. Out of fifteen symbols in the first message, four were the same, so it was reasonable to set this down as E. In some cases the figure was bearing a flag, and it was probable, from the way in which the flags were distributed, that they were used to break the sentence up into words. I accepted this as a hypothesis.

"But now came the real difficulty of the inquiry. The order of the English letters after E is by no means well marked. Speaking roughly, T, A, O, I, N, S, H, R, D, and L are the numerical order in which letters occur; but T, A, O, and I are very nearly abreast of each other, and it would be an endless task to try each combination until a meaning was arrived at. I therefore waited for fresh material. In my second interview with Mr. Hilton Cubitt he was able to give me two other short sentences and one message, which appeared—since there was no flag—to be a single word. Here are the symbols. Now, in the single word I have already got the two E's coming second and fourth in a word of five letters. It might be 'sever,' or 'lever,' or 'never.' There can be no question that the latter as a reply to an appeal is far the most probable, and the circumstances pointed to its being a reply written by the lady. Accepting it as correct, we are now able to say that the symbols ⚑┤╞ stand respectively for N, V, and R.

"Now it occurred to me that if these appeals came, as I expected, from someone who had been intimate with the lady in her early life, a combination which contained two E's with three letters between might very well stand for the name ELSIE. I found on examination that such a combination formed the termination of the message which was three times repeated. It was certainly some appeal to Elsie. In this way I had got my L, S, and I. But what appeal could it be? There were only four letters in the word which preceded Elsie, and it ended in E. Surely the word must be COME. I tried all other four letters ending in E, but could find none to fit the case. So now I was in possession of C, O, and M, and I was in a position to attack the first message once more, dividing it into words and putting dots for each symbol which was still unknown. So treated, it worked out in this fashion:

.M .ERE . .E SL.NE.

"Now the first letter *can* only be A, which is a useful discovery, since it occurs no fewer than three times in this short sentence, and the H is also apparent in the second word. Now it becomes:

AM HERE A.E SLANE.

Or, filling in the vacancies in the name:

AM HERE ABE SLANEY

"I had so many letters now that I could proceed with considerable confidence to the second message, which worked out in this fashion:

A. ELRI.ES

Here I could only make sense by putting T and G for the missing letters, and supposing that the name was that of some house or inn at which the writer was staying."

Inspector Martin and I had listened with the utmost interest to the full and clear account of how my friend had produced results which had led to so complete a command over our difficulties.

"What did you do then, sir?" asked the inspector.

"I supposed that this Abe Slaney was an American, since Abe is an American contraction, and since a letter from America had been the starting point of all the trouble. I also thought there was some criminal secret in the matter. The lady's allusions to

44

her past, and her refusal to take her husband into her confidence, both pointed in that direction. I therefore cabled to Wilson Hargreave, of the New York Police Bureau, who has more than once made use of my knowledge of London crime. I asked him whether the name of Abe Slaney was known to him. Here is his reply:

THE MOST DANGEROUS CROOK IN CHICAGO.

"On the very evening upon which I had his answer, Hilton Cubitt sent me the last message from Slaney. Working with known letters, it took this form:

ELSIE .RE.ARE TO MEET THY GO.

The addition of a P and a D completed a message which showed me that the rascal was proceeding from persuasion to threats, and my knowledge of the crooks of Chicago prepared me to find that he might very rapidly put his words into action. I at once came to Norfolk with my friend, Dr. Watson, but, unhappily, only in time to find that the worst had already occurred."

"It is a privilege to be associated with you in the handling of a case," said the inspector warmly. "You will excuse me, however, if I speak frankly. You are only answerable to yourself, but I have to answer to my superiors. If this Abe Slaney, living at Elrige's, is indeed the murderer, and if he has made his escape while I am seated here, I should certainly get into serious trouble."

"You need not be uneasy. He will not try to escape. To do so would be a confession of guilt."

"Then let us go to arrest him."

"I expect him here every instant."

"But why should he come?"

"Because I have written and asked him."

"But this is incredible, Mr. Holmes! Why should he come because you have asked him? Would not such a request rouse his suspicions and cause him to fly?"

"I think I have known how to frame the letter," said Holmes. "And, if I am not mistaken, here is the gentleman himself coming up the drive."

A man was striding up the path to the door. He was a tall, handsome, swarthy fellow, clad in a suit of gray flannel, with a Panama hat, a bristling black beard, and flourishing a cane. He swaggered up the path as if the place belonged to him, and we heard his loud, confident peal at the bell.

"I think, gentlemen," said Holmes quietly, "that we had best take up our position behind the door. Every precaution is necessary when dealing with such a fellow. You will need your handcuffs, Inspector. You can leave the talking to me."

We waited in silence for a minute—one of those minutes which one can never forget. Then the door opened and the man stepped in. In an instant Holmes clapped a pistol to his head, and Martin slipped the handcuffs over his wrists. It was all done so swiftly that the fellow was helpless before he knew that he was attacked. He glared from one to the other of us with blazing black eyes. Then he burst into a bitter laugh. "Well, gentlemen, you have the drop on me. I seem to have knocked up against something hard. But I came in answer to a letter from Mrs. Hilton Cubitt. Don't tell me that she set a trap for me?"

"Mrs. Hilton Cubitt was seriously injured, and is near death."

The man gave a hoarse cry of grief. "You're crazy! It was he that was hurt, not she. I may have threatened her—God forgive me!—but I would not have touched a hair of her pretty head. Take it back! Say that she is not hurt!"

"She was found, badly wounded, beside her dead husband."

He sank with a deep groan onto the settee, and buried his face in his manacled hands. For five minutes he was silent. Then he raised his face once more, and spoke with the cold composure of despair. "I have nothing to hide from you, gentlemen," said he. "If I shot the man he had his shot at me, and there's no murder in that. But I couldn't have hurt that woman. I tell you, there was never a man in this world loved a woman more than I loved her. She was pledged to me years ago. Who was this Englishman that he should come between us? I tell you that I had the first right to her, and that I was only claiming my own."

"She broke away from your influence when she found the man

that you are," said Holmes sternly. "She fled from America to avoid you, and she married an honorable gentleman in England. You followed her and made her life a misery, in order to induce her to abandon the husband whom she loved and respected and fly with you, whom she feared and hated. You have ended by bringing about his death and driving her to suicide."

"If Elsie dies, I care nothing what becomes of me," said the American. He opened one of his hands, and looked at a note crumpled up in his palm. "See here, mister," he cried, with a gleam of suspicion in his eyes, "you're not trying to scare me over this, are you? If the lady is hurt as bad as you say, who was it that wrote this note?" He tossed it forward onto the table.

"I wrote it, to bring you here."

"You wrote it? There was no one on earth outside the Joint who knew the secret of the dancing men."

"What one man can invent another can discover," said Holmes. "There is a cab coming to convey you to Norwich, Mr. Slaney. But, meanwhile, you have time to make some small reparation for the injury you have wrought. Are you aware that Mrs. Hilton Cubitt has herself lain under grave suspicion of the murder of her husband? The least that you owe her is to make it clear to the world that she was in no way responsible for his tragic end."

"I ask nothing better," said the American. "I guess the very best case I can make for myself is the absolute naked truth."

"It is my duty to warn you that it will be used against you," cried the inspector, with the magnificent fair play of the British criminal law.

Slaney shrugged. "I'll chance that," said he. "First of all, I want you gentlemen to understand that I have known this lady since she was a child. There were seven of us in a gang in Chicago, and Elsie's father was the boss of the Joint. He was a clever man, was old Patrick. It was he who invented that writing, which would pass as a child's scrawl unless you had the key to it. Well, Elsie learned some of our ways, but she couldn't stand the business, and she had a bit of honest money of her own, so she gave us all the slip and got away to London. She had been engaged to me, and she would have married me, I believe, if I had taken over another profession, but she would have nothing to do with anything on the cross. It was only after her marriage to this Englishman that I was able to find out where she was. I wrote to her, but got no answer. After that I came over, and, as letters were no use, I put my messages where she could read them.

"Well, I have been here a month now. I lived at that farm, where I had a room down below, and could get in and out every night, and no one the wiser. I tried all I could to coax Elsie away. I knew that she read the messages, for once she wrote an answer under one of them. Then my temper got the better of me, and I began to threaten her. She sent me a letter then, imploring me to go away, and saying that it would break her heart if any scandal should come upon her husband. She said that she would come down when her husband was asleep at three in the morning, and speak with me through the end window, if I would go away afterwards and leave her in peace. She came down and brought money with her, trying to bribe me to go. This made me mad, and I caught her arm and tried to pull her through the window. At that moment in rushed the husband with his revolver in his hand. Elsie had sunk down upon the floor, and we were face to face. I held up my gun to scare him off and let me get away. He fired and missed me. I pulled off almost at the same instant, and down he dropped. As I made away across the garden, I heard the window shut behind me. That's God's truth, gentlemen, every word of it."

A cab had driven up whilst the American had been talking. Two uniformed policemen sat inside. Inspector Martin rose and touched his prisoner on the shoulder. "It is time for us to go."

"Can I see her first?"

"No, she is not conscious. Mr. Sherlock Holmes, I only hope that, if ever again I have an important case, I shall have the good fortune to have you by my side."

We stood at the window and watched the cab drive away. As I turned back, my eye caught the pellet of paper which the prisoner had tossed upon the table. It was the note with which Holmes had decoyed him.

"See if you can read it, Watson," said he, with a smile.

It contained no word, but this little line of dancing men:

"If you use the code which I have explained," said Holmes, "you will find that it simply means, COME HERE AT ONCE. I was convinced that it was an invitation which he would not refuse, since he could never imagine that it could come from anyone but the lady. And so, my dear Watson, we have ended by turning the dancing men to good when they have so often been the agents of evil. Three forty is our train, and I fancy we should be back in Baker Street for dinner."

ONLY ONE WORD OF EPILOGUE. The American, Abe Slaney, was condemned to death at the winter assizes at Norwich, but his penalty was changed to penal servitude in consideration of mitigating circumstances, and the certainty that Hilton Cubitt had fired the first shot. Of Mrs. Hilton Cubitt I only know that I have heard she recovered entirely, and that she still remains a widow, devoting her whole life to the care of the poor and to the administration of her husband's estate.

Silver Blaze

"I AM AFRAID, WATSON, that I shall have to go," said Holmes, as we sat down together to our breakfast one morning.

"Go! Where to?"

"To Dartmoor—to King's Pyland."

I was not surprised. Indeed, my only wonder was that he had not already been mixed up in this extraordinary case, which was the one topic of conversation through the length and breadth of England. For a whole day my companion had rambled about the room with his chin upon his chest and his brows knitted, charging and recharging his pipe with the strongest black tobacco, and absolutely deaf to any of my questions or remarks. Fresh editions of every paper had been sent up by our news agent, only to be glanced over and tossed into a corner. Yet, silent as he was, I knew perfectly well what it was over which he was brooding. There was but one problem before the public which could challenge his powers of analysis, and that was the singular disappearance of the favorite for the Wessex Cup, and the tragic murder of its trainer.

"I should be most happy to go down with you if I should not be in the way," said I.

"My dear Watson, you would confer a great favor upon me by coming. We have just time to catch our train at Paddington, and you would oblige me by bringing with you your excellent field glass."

An hour or so later I found myself in a first-class carriage, flying along, en route for Exeter, while Sherlock Holmes, with his sharp, eager face framed in his ear-flapped traveling cap, dipped rapidly into the bundle of fresh papers which he had procured at Paddington. We had left Reading far behind us before he thrust the last of them under the seat, and offered me his cigar case.

"I presume," said he, "that you have already read of the murder of John Straker and the disappearance of Silver Blaze?"

"I have seen what the *Telegraph* and the *Chronicle* have to say."

"The difficulty in this case is to detach the framework of fact—of absolute, undeniable fact—from the embellishments of the theorists and reporters, and to see which are the special points upon which the whole mystery turns. On Tuesday evening I received telegrams from both Colonel Ross, the owner of the horse, and from Inspector Gregory, who is looking after the case, inviting my cooperation."

"Tuesday evening!" I exclaimed. "And this is Thursday morning. Why did you not go down yesterday?"

"Because I made a blunder, my dear Watson—which is, I am afraid, a more common occurrence than anyone would think who only knew me through your memoirs. I could not believe that the most remarkable horse in England could long remain concealed, especially in so sparsely inhabited a place as Dartmoor. From hour to hour yesterday I expected to hear that he had been found, and that his abductor was the murderer of John Straker. When another morning had come and, beyond the arrest of young Fitzroy Simpson, nothing had been done, I felt that it was time to take action."

"You have formed a theory then?"

"At least I have a grip of the essential facts of the case. I shall enumerate them to you, for nothing clears up a case so much as stating it to another person."

I lay back against the cushions, puffing at my cigar, while Holmes, leaning forward, with his long thin forefinger checking off the points upon the palm of his left hand, gave me a sketch of the events which had led to our journey.

"Silver Blaze," said he, "holds a brilliant record. He is now in his fifth year, and has brought in turn each of the prizes of the turf to Colonel Ross, his fortunate owner. Up to the time of the catastrophe he was first favorite for the Wessex Cup, the betting being three to one on. He has never yet disappointed the racing public, so that even at short odds enormous sums of money have been laid upon him. It is obvious, therefore, that many people had the strongest interest in preventing Silver Blaze from being there at the fall of the flag next Tuesday.

"This fact was, of course, appreciated at King's Pyland, where the colonel's training stable is situated. Every precaution was taken to guard the favorite. The trainer, John Straker, was a retired jockey, who rode in Colonel Ross's colors before he became too heavy for the weighing chair. He served the colonel for five years as jockey, and for seven as trainer. Under him were three lads, one of whom sat up each night in the stable, while the others slept in the loft. John Straker, who was a married man, lived in a small villa about two hundred yards from the stables. The country round is very lonely, but about half a mile to the north there is a small cluster of villas built for the use of invalids and others who may wish to enjoy the pure Dartmoor air. Tavistock lies two miles to the west, while across the moor, also about two miles distant, is the larger training establishment of Capleton, which belongs to Lord Backwater, and is managed by Silas Brown. In every other direction the moor is a wilderness, inhabited only by a few roaming gypsies.

"Last Monday evening the horses had been exercised and watered as usual, and the stables were locked up at nine o'clock. Two of the lads walked up to the trainer's house, where they had supper in the kitchen, while the third, Ned Hunter, remained on guard. At a few minutes after nine the maid, Edith Baxter, carried down to the stables his supper, which consisted of a dish of curried mutton. She carried a lantern with her, as it was very dark and the path ran across the open moor. Edith Baxter was within thirty yards of the stables when a man appeared out of the darkness and called to her to stop. As he stepped into the circle of light thrown by the lantern she saw that he was a person of gentlemanly bearing, dressed in a gray suit of tweed with a cloth cap. He wore gaiters, and carried a heavy stick with a knob to it. She was most impressed, however, by the extreme pallor of his face and by the nervousness of his manner.

"'Can you tell me where I am?' he asked. 'I had almost made up my mind to sleep on the moor when I saw your light.'

"'You are close to the King's Pyland stables,' she said.

"'Oh, indeed! What a stroke of luck!' he cried. 'Perhaps that is the stableboy's supper which you are carrying to him. Now I am sure that you would not be too proud to earn the price of a new dress, would you?' He took a folded piece of paper out of his waistcoat pocket. 'See that the boy has this tonight, and you shall have the prettiest frock that money can buy.'

"She was frightened by the earnestness of his manner, and ran past him to the window through which she was accustomed to hand the meals. It was already open, and Hunter was seated at the small table inside. She had begun to tell him of what had happened, when the stranger came up again.

"'Good evening,' said he, looking through the window. 'I wanted to have a word with you.'

"'What business have you here?' asked the lad.

"'It's business that may put something into your pocket,' said the other. 'You've two horses in for the Wessex Cup—Silver Blaze and Bayard. Let me have the straight tip, and you won't be a loser. Is it a fact that at the weights Bayard could give the other a hundred yards in five furlongs, and that the stable have put their money on him?'

"'So you're one of those damned touts,' cried the lad. 'I'll show you how we serve them in King's Pyland.' He sprang up and rushed across the stable to unloose the dog. The girl fled away to the house, but as she ran she looked back, and saw that the stranger was leaning through the window. A minute later, however, when Hunter rushed out with the hound he was gone, and the lad failed to find any trace of him."

"One moment!" I asked. "Did the stableboy, when he ran out with the dog, leave the door unlocked behind him?"

"Excellent, Watson, excellent!" murmured my companion. "The importance of the point struck me so forcibly that I sent a special wire to Dartmoor yesterday to clear the matter up. The boy locked the door before he left it. The window, I may add, was not large enough for a man to get through.

"Hunter waited until his fellow grooms had returned, when he sent a message up to the trainer and told him what had occurred. Straker does not seem to have quite realized the true significance of the account. It left him, however, vaguely uneasy, and Mrs. Straker, waking at one in the morning, found that he was dressing. He said that he could not sleep on account of his anxiety about the horses, and that he intended to walk down to the stables to see that all was well. She begged him to remain at home, as she could hear the rain pattering against the windows, but he pulled on his mackintosh and left the house.

"Mrs. Straker awoke at seven in the morning to find that he had not yet returned. She dressed hastily, called the maid, and set off for the stables. The door was open; inside, huddled upon a chair, Hunter was sunk in a state of absolute stupor, the favorite's stall was empty, and there were no signs of his trainer.

"The two lads who slept in the loft were quickly roused. They had heard nothing during the night, for they are both sound sleepers. Hunter was obviously under the influence of some powerful drug; and he was left to sleep it off while the two lads and the two women ran out in search of the absentees. They still hoped that the trainer had for some reason taken out the horse for early exercise, but on ascending the knoll near the house, from which all the neighboring moors were visible, they perceived something which warned them that they were in the presence of a tragedy.

"About a quarter of a mile from the stables, John Straker's overcoat was flapping from a furze bush. Immediately beyond there was a bowl-shaped depression in the moor, and at the bottom of this was found his dead body. His head had been shattered by a savage blow from some heavy weapon, and he was wounded in the thigh, where there was a long, clean cut, inflicted evidently by some very sharp instrument. It was clear that Straker had defended himself vigorously against his assailants, for in his right hand he held a small knife, which was clotted with blood up to the handle, while in his left he grasped a red and black silk cravat, which was recognized by the maid as having been worn on the preceding evening by the stranger who had visited the stables.

"Hunter, on recovering from his stupor, was also positive as to the ownership of the cravat. He was equally certain that the same stranger had, while standing at the window, drugged his curried mutton, and so deprived the stables of their watchman.

"As to the missing horse, there were abundant proofs in the mud which lay at the bottom of the fatal hollow that he had been there at the time of the struggle. But from that moment he has disappeared; and although a large reward has been offered, no news has come of him. Finally, an analysis has shown that the remains of his supper, left by the stableboy, contain an appreciable quantity of powdered opium, while the people of the house partook of the same dish on the same night without any ill effect.

"Those are the main facts of the case stripped of all surmise and stated as baldly as possible. I shall now recapitulate what the police have done. Inspector Gregory, to whom the case has been committed, is an extremely competent officer. Were he but gifted with imagination he might rise to great heights in his profession. On his arrival he promptly found and arrested the man upon whom suspicion naturally rested. There was little difficulty in finding him, for he was thoroughly well-known in the neighborhood. His name, it appears, was Fitzroy Simpson. He was a man of excellent birth and education, who had squandered a fortune upon the turf, and who lived by doing a little quiet and genteel bookmaking in the sporting clubs of London. An examination of his betting book shows that bets to the amount of five thousand pounds had been registered by him against the favorite.

"On being arrested he stated that he had come down to Dartmoor in the hope of getting some information about the King's Pyland horses, and also about Desborough, the second favorite, which was in charge of Silas Brown, at the Capleton stables. He did not deny that he had acted as described upon the evening before, but declared that he had simply wished to obtain firsthand information. When confronted with the cravat he turned pale, and was unable to account for its presence in the hand of the murdered man. His wet clothing showed that he had been out in the storm of the night before, and his stick, which was weighted with lead, was just such a weapon as might, by repeated blows, have inflicted the terrible injuries to which the trainer had succumbed. On the other hand, there was no wound upon his person, while the state of Straker's knife would show that one, at least, of his assailants must bear his mark upon him."

"Is it not possible," I suggested, "that the incised wound upon Straker may have been caused by his own knife in the convulsive struggles which follow any brain injury?"

"It is more than possible; it is probable," said Holmes. "In that case, one of the main points in favor of the accused disappears. The police imagine, in fact, that, having drugged the lad, and having in some way obtained a duplicate key, he opened the stable door, and took out the horse, with the intention of kidnaping him. His bridle is missing, so that Simpson must have put it on. Then, having left the door open behind him, he was leading the horse away over the moor, when he was overtaken by the trainer. A row naturally ensued. Simpson beat out the trainer's brains with his heavy stick without receiving any injury from the small knife which Straker used in self-defense, and then the thief either led the horse on to some secret hiding place, or else it may have bolted during the struggle, and be now wandering out on the moors. That is the case as it appears to the police, and improbable as it is, all other explanations are more improbable still."

IT WAS EVENING BEFORE WE REACHED the little town of Tavistock, which lies, like the boss of a shield, in the middle of the huge circle of Dartmoor. Two gentlemen were awaiting us at the station: the one a tall, fair man with lionlike hair and beard, and curiously penetrating light blue eyes; the other a small, alert person, very neat and dapper, in a frock coat and gaiters, with trim little side-whiskers and an eyeglass. The latter was Colonel Ross, the well-known sportsman, the other Inspector Gregory, a man who was rapidly making his name in the English detective service.

"I am delighted that you have come down, Mr. Holmes," said the colonel. "I wish to leave no stone unturned in trying to avenge poor Straker, and in recovering my horse."

"We have an open carriage outside," said the inspector, "and as you would no doubt like to see the place before the light fails, we might talk as we drive."

A minute later we were all seated in a comfortable landau and were rattling through the quaint old Devonshire town. "The net is drawn pretty close round Fitzroy Simpson," Gregory remarked, "and I believe myself that he is our man. At the same time, I recognize that the evidence is purely circumstantial."

"How about Straker's knife?" asked Holmes.

"We have concluded that he wounded himself in his fall."

"My friend Dr. Watson made that suggestion to me as we came down."

"Simpson has neither a knife nor any sign of a wound. Still, he had a great interest in the disappearance of the favorite, he lies under the suspicion of having poisoned the stableboy, he was undoubtedly out in the storm, he was armed with a heavy stick, and his cravat was found in the dead man's hand. I really think we have enough to go before a jury."

Holmes shook his head. "A clever counsel would tear it all to rags. Why should he take the horse out of the stable? If he wished to injure it, why could he not do it there? Has a duplicate key been found in his possession? What chemist sold him the powdered opium? What is his explanation as to the paper which he wished the maid to give to the stableboy?"

"He says it was a ten-pound note. One was found in his purse. But your other difficulties are not so formidable as they seem. The opium was probably brought from London. The key, having served its purpose, would be hurled away. The horse may lie at the bottom of one of the old mine pits upon the moor."

"What does he say about the cravat?"

"He acknowledges that it is his, and declares that he had lost it. But a new element has been introduced into the case which may account for his leading the horse from the stable."

Holmes pricked up his ears.

"We have found traces which show that a party of gypsies encamped on Monday night within a mile of the spot where the murder took place. On Tuesday they were gone. Now, presuming that there was some understanding between Simpson and these gypsies, might he not have been leading the horse to them when he was overtaken, and may they not have him now?"

"It is certainly possible."

"The moor is being scoured for these gypsies. I have also examined every stable and outbuilding for a radius of ten miles."

"There is another training stable quite close, I understand?"

"Yes, and as Desborough, their horse, was second in the betting, they had an interest in the disappearance of the favorite. Silas Brown, the trainer, had large bets upon the event, and he was no friend of poor Straker. We have, however, examined the stables, and there is nothing to connect him with the affair."

"And nothing to connect this man Simpson with the interests of the Capleton stables?"

"Nothing at all."

Holmes leaned back in the carriage and the conversation ceased. A few minutes later our driver pulled up at a neat little red-brick villa with overhanging eaves, which stood by the road. Some distance off, across a paddock, lay a long gray-tiled outbuilding. In every other direction the low curves of the moor, bronze-colored from the fading ferns, stretched away to the skyline, broken only by the steeples of Tavistock, and by a cluster of houses away to the westward, which marked the Capleton stables. We all sprang out with the exception of Holmes, who continued absorbed in his own thoughts until I touched his arm, when he roused himself with a start and stepped out of the carriage.

"Excuse me," said he, turning to Colonel Ross, who had looked at him in some surprise. "I was daydreaming." There was a gleam in his eyes and a suppressed excitement in his manner which convinced me, used as I was to his ways, that his hand was upon a clue, though I could not imagine where he had found it.

"Perhaps you would prefer at once to go on to the scene of the crime, Mr. Holmes?" said Gregory.

"I think I should prefer to stay here a little and go into one or two questions of detail. I presume that you made an inventory of what Straker had in his pockets at the time of his death?"

"I have the things themselves in the sitting room."

We all filed into the front room, and sat round the central table, while the inspector unlocked a square tin box and laid a small heap of things before us. There was a box of matches, two inches of tallow candle, a briar pipe, a pouch of sealskin with half an ounce of tobacco, a silver watch with a gold chain, five gold sovereigns, an aluminum pencil case, a few papers, and an ivory-handled knife with a delicate inflexible blade.

"This is a very singular knife," said Holmes, lifting it up and examining it minutely. "I presume, as I see bloodstains upon it, that it is the one which was found in the dead man's grasp. Watson, this knife is surely in your line."

"It is what we call a cataract knife," said I.

"I thought so. A very delicate blade devised for very delicate work. A strange thing for a man to carry with him upon a rough expedition, especially as it would not shut in his pocket."

"The tip was guarded by a cork which we found beside his body," said the inspector. "His wife tells us that the knife had lain for some days upon the dressing table, and that he had picked it up as he left the room. It was a poor weapon, but perhaps the best that he could lay his hand on at the moment."

"Very possible. How about these papers?"

"Three of them are receipted hay dealers' accounts. One of them is a letter of instructions from Colonel Ross. This other is a dressmaker's account for thirty-seven pounds fifteen, made out by Madame Lesurier, of Bond Street, to William Darbyshire. Mrs. Straker tells us that Darbyshire was a friend of her husband's, and that occasionally his letters were addressed here."

"Madame Darbyshire has expensive tastes," remarked Holmes, glancing down the account. "Twenty-two guineas is rather heavy for a single costume. However, there appears to be nothing more to learn, and we may now go to the scene of the crime."

As we emerged from the sitting room a woman who had been waiting in the passage took a step forward and laid her hand upon the inspector's sleeve. Her face was haggard and eager.

"Have you got them? Have you found them?" she panted.

"No, Mrs. Straker; but Mr. Holmes, here, has come from London to help us, and we shall do all that is possible."

"Surely I met you in Plymouth, at a garden party, some little time ago, Mrs. Straker," said Holmes.

"No, sir; you are mistaken."

"Dear me; why, I could have sworn to it. You wore a costume of dove-colored silk with ostrich-feather trimming."

"I never had such a dress, sir," answered the lady.

"Ah, that quite settles it," said Holmes, and, with an apology, he followed the inspector outside. A short walk across the moor took us to the hollow in which the body had been found. At the brink of it was the bush upon which the coat had been hung.

"I perceive that the ground has been trampled up a good deal," said Holmes. "No doubt many feet have been here since Monday."

"A piece of matting has been laid here at the side, and we have all stood upon that."

"Excellent."

"In this bag I have one of the boots which Straker wore, one of Fitzroy Simpson's shoes, and a cast horseshoe of Silver Blaze."

"My dear Inspector, you surpass yourself!"

Holmes took the bag, and descending into the hollow he pushed the matting into a more central position. Then stretching himself upon his face and leaning his chin upon his hands, he made a careful study of the trampled mud in front of him.

"Halloa!" said he suddenly. "What's this?"

It was a wax match, half burned, which was so coated with mud that it looked at first like a little chip of wood.

"I cannot think how I came to overlook it," said the inspector, with an expression of annoyance.

"It was invisible, buried in the mud. I only saw it because I was looking for it."

"What! You expected to find it?"

"I thought it not unlikely." Holmes took the boot and shoe from the bag and compared the impressions of each of them with marks upon the ground. Then he clambered up to the rim of the hollow and crawled about among the ferns and bushes.

"I am afraid that there are no more tracks," said the inspector. "I have examined the ground very carefully for a hundred yards in each direction."

"Indeed!" said Holmes, rising. "I should not have the impertinence to do it again after what you say. But I should like to take a little walk over the moors before it grows dark, and I think that I shall put this horseshoe into my pocket for luck."

Colonel Ross, who had shown some signs of impatience at my companion's quiet and systematic method of work, glanced at his watch. "I wish you would come back with me, Inspector," said he. "There are several points on which I should like your advice, and especially as to whether we do not owe it to the public to remove our horse's name from the entries for the Cup."

"Certainly not," cried Holmes. "I should let the name stand."

The colonel bowed. "I am very glad to have had your opinion, sir," said he. "You will find us at poor Straker's house when you have finished your walk, and we can drive together into Tavistock."

He turned back with the inspector, while Holmes and I walked slowly across the moor. The sun was beginning to sink behind the stables of Capleton, and the landscape was glorious in the evening light; but it was all wasted upon my companion, who was sunk in the deepest thought.

"It's this way, Watson," he said at last. "We may leave the question of who killed John Straker for the instant, and confine ourselves to finding out what has become of the horse. Now, supposing that he broke away during or after the tragedy, where could he have gone to? The horse is a gregarious creature. If left to himself, his instincts would have been either to return to King's Pyland or go over to Capleton. Why should he run wild upon the moor? And why should gypsies kidnap him? These people always clear out when they hear of trouble, for they do not wish to be pestered by the police. They could not hope to sell such a horse. They would run a great risk and gain nothing by taking him."

"Where is he, then?"

"I have already said that he must have gone to King's Pyland or to Capleton. He is not at King's Pyland, therefore he is at Capleton. Let us take that as a working hypothesis, and see what it leads us to. This part of the moor is very hard and dry. But it falls away towards Capleton, and you can see that there is a long hollow over yonder, which must have been very wet on Monday night. If our supposition is correct, then the horse must have crossed that, and there is where we should look for his tracks."

We had been walking briskly during this conversation, and a few more minutes brought us to the hollow in question. At Holmes's request I walked down the bank to the right, and he to the left, but I had not taken fifty paces before I heard him give a shout, and saw him waving to me. The track of a horse was plainly outlined in the soft earth in front of him, and the shoe he took from his pocket exactly fitted the impression. "See the value of imagination," said he. "It is the one quality which Gregory lacks. We imagined what might have happened, acted upon the supposition, and find ourselves justified. Let us proceed."

We crossed the marshy bottom and passed over a quarter of a mile of dry, hard turf. Again the ground sloped and again we came on the tracks. Then we lost them for half a mile, but only to pick them up once more quite close to Capleton. Here, a man's track was visible beside the horse's. The double track turned sharp off and took the direction of King's Pyland. Holmes whistled, and we both followed along after it. His eyes were on the trail, but I happened to look a little to one side, and saw to my surprise the same tracks coming back again in the opposite direction.

"One for you, Watson," said Holmes, when I pointed it out. "You have saved us a long walk which would have brought us back on our own traces. Let us follow the return track."

We had not to go far. It ended at the paving of asphalt which led up to the gates of the Capleton stables. As we approached them a groom ran out. "We don't want any loiterers here," said he.

"I only wished to ask a question," said Holmes. "Should I be too early to see your master, Mr. Silas Brown, if I were to call at five o'clock tomorrow morning?"

"If anyone is about he will be, sir, for he is always the first stirring. But here he is to answer for himself."

A fierce-looking elderly man was striding out from the gate with a hunting crop swinging in his hand. "What's this, Dawson?" he cried. "No gossiping! Go about your business! And you—what the devil do you want here?"

"Ten minutes' talk with you, my good sir," said Holmes in the sweetest of voices.

"I've no time to talk to every gadabout. We want no strangers here. Be off, or you may find a dog at your heels."

Holmes leaned forward and whispered something in the trainer's ear. He started violently and flushed to the temples. "It's a lie!" he shouted. "An infernal lie!"

"Shall we argue about it here, or talk it over in your parlor?"

"Oh, come in if you wish to."

Holmes smiled. "I shall not keep you more than a few minutes, Watson," he said. "Now, Mr. Brown, I am at your disposal."

It was quite twenty minutes before Holmes and the trainer reappeared. Never have I seen such a change as had been brought about in Silas Brown in that short time. His face was ashy pale, beads of perspiration shone upon his brow, and his hands shook until the hunting crop wagged like a branch in the wind. His bullying manner was all gone, and he cringed along at my companion's side like a dog with its master. "Your instructions will be done," said he. "You can rely upon me."

"Yes, I think I can. Well, you shall hear from me tomorrow." Holmes turned upon his heel, disregarding the trembling hand which the other held out to him, and we set off together for King's Pyland.

"A more perfect compound of the bully, coward and sneak than Master Silas Brown I have seldom met with," remarked Holmes.

"He has the horse, then?"

"He tried to bluster out of it, but I described to him so exactly what his actions had been upon that morning, that he is convinced that I was watching him. Of course, you observed the peculiarly square toes in the impressions, and that his own boots exactly corresponded to them. Again, of course, no subordinate would have dared to have done such a thing. I described to him how when, according to his custom, he was the first down, he perceived a strange horse wandering over the moor; how he went out to it, and his astonishment at recognizing from the white forehead which has given the favorite its name that chance had put in his power the only horse which could beat the one upon which he had put his money. Then I described how his first impulse had been to lead him back to King's Pyland, and how the devil had shown him how he could hide the horse until after the race, and how he had led it back and concealed it at Capleton. When I told him all this he gave it up, and thought only of saving his own skin."

"But his stables had been searched."

"Oh, an old horse faker like him has many a dodge."

"But are you not afraid to leave the horse in his power now, since he has every interest in injuring it?"

"My dear fellow, he will guard it as the apple of his eye. He knows that his only hope of mercy is to produce it safe."

"Colonel Ross did not impress me as a man who would be likely to show much mercy in any case."

"The matter does not rest with Colonel Ross. I tell as much or as little as I choose. That is the advantage of being unofficial. I don't know whether you observed it, Watson, but the colonel's manner has been just a trifle cavalier to me. I am inclined now to have a little amusement at his expense. Say nothing to him about the horse. And, of course, this is all quite a minor case compared with the question of who killed John Straker."

"And you will devote yourself to that?"

"On the contrary, we both go back to London by the night train."

I was thunderstruck; but not a word more could I draw from him until we were back at the trainer's house. The colonel and the inspector were awaiting us in the parlor.

"My friend and I return to town by the midnight express," said Holmes. "We have had a charming little breath of your beautiful Dartmoor air."

The inspector opened his eyes, and the colonel's lips curled in a sneer. "So you despair of arresting the murderer," said he.

"There are certainly grave difficulties in the way," said Holmes. "I have every hope, however, that your horse will start upon Tuesday, and I beg that you will have your jockey in readiness. Might I ask for a photograph of Mr. John Straker?"

The inspector took one from an envelope in his pocket and handed it to him.

"My dear Gregory, you anticipate all my wants. Now, I have a question which I should like to put to the maid."

"I must say that I am rather disappointed in our London consultant," said Colonel Ross bluntly, as my friend left the room. "I do not see that we are any further than when he came."

I was about to make some reply in defense of my friend, when he entered the room again. "Now, gentlemen," said he, "I am quite ready for Tavistock."

As we stepped into the carriage one of the stableboys held the door open for us. A sudden idea seemed to occur to Holmes, for he leaned forward and touched the lad upon the sleeve. "You have a few sheep in the paddock," he said. "Have you noticed anything amiss with them of late?"

"Well, sir, not much, but three of them have gone lame."

Holmes chuckled and rubbed his hands together. "A long shot, Watson; a very long shot!" said he, pinching my arm. "Gregory, let me recommend to your attention this singular epidemic among the sheep. Drive on, coachman!"

I saw by the inspector's face that his attention had been keenly aroused. "You consider that to be important?" he asked.

"Exceedingly so. I also wish to draw your attention to the curious incident of the dog in the nighttime."

"The dog did nothing in the nighttime."

"That was the curious incident," remarked Sherlock Holmes.

FOUR DAYS LATER HOLMES AND I were in the train bound for Winchester, to see the race for the Wessex Cup. Colonel Ross met us, by appointment, at the station, and we drove in his drag to the course beyond the town. His face was grave and his manner cold in the extreme.

"I have seen nothing of my horse," said he.

"I suppose you would know him when you saw him?" asked Holmes.

The colonel was very angry. "A child would know Silver Blaze with his white forehead and his mottled off foreleg," said he.

"How is the betting?"

"Well, that is the curious part of it. You could have got fifteen to one yesterday, but the price has become shorter and shorter, until you can hardly get three to one now."

"Hum!" said Holmes. "Somebody knows something!"

As we drew up in the enclosure near the grandstand, I glanced at the card and saw there were six entries including Silver Blaze.

"We have put all hopes on your word," said the colonel. "Why, what is that? Silver Blaze favorite?"

"Five to four against Silver Blaze!" roared the ring. "Fifteen to five against Desborough! Five to four on the field!"

"There are the numbers up," I cried. "They are all six there."

"All six there! Then my horse is running," cried the colonel in great agitation. "But I don't see him."

"Only five have passed. This must be he."

As I spoke a powerful bay horse swept out from the weighing enclosure and cantered past us, bearing on its back the well-known black and red colors of the colonel's stables.

"That's not my horse," cried the owner. "That beast has not a white hair upon its body. What is this that you have done, Mr. Holmes?"

"Well, well, let us see how he gets on," said my friend imperturbably. For a few minutes he gazed through my field glass. "Capital! An excellent start!" he cried suddenly. "There they are, coming round the curve!"

From our drag we had a superb view as the six horses came up the straight. They were so close together that a carpet could have covered them, but halfway up the yellow of the Capleton stables showed to the front. Before they reached us, however,

Desborough's bolt was shot, and the colonel's horse, coming away with a rush, passed the post six lengths before its rival.

"It's my race anyhow," gasped the colonel, passing his hand over his eyes, "but I can make neither head nor tail of it. Haven't you kept up your mystery long enough, Mr. Holmes?"

"Certainly, Colonel. You shall know everything. Let us all go round and have a look at the horse together. Here he is," he continued, as we made our way into the weighing enclosure. "You have only to wash his face and his leg in spirits of wine and you will find that he is the same old Silver Blaze as ever. I found him in the hands of a faker, and took the liberty of running him just as he was sent over."

"My dear sir, you have done wonders. The horse looks very fit and well. It never went better in its life. I owe you a thousand apologies for having doubted your ability. You have done me a great service by recovering my horse. You would do me a greater still if you could lay your hands on the murderer of John Straker."

"I have done so," said Holmes quietly.

The colonel and I stared at him in amazement. "You have got him! Where is he, then?"

"He is here."

"Here! Where?"

"In my company."

The colonel flushed angrily. "I quite recognize that I am under obligations to you, Mr. Holmes," said he, "but I must regard what you have just said as either a very bad joke or an insult."

Sherlock Holmes laughed. "I assure you that I have not associated you with the crime, Colonel," said he. "The real murderer is standing immediately behind you!" He stepped past and laid his hand upon the glossy neck of the Thoroughbred.

"The horse!" cried both the colonel and myself.

"Yes, the horse. And it may lessen his guilt if I say that it was done in self-defense, and that John Straker was a man who was entirely unworthy of your confidence. But there goes the bell; and as I stand to win a little on this next race, I shall defer a more lengthy explanation until a more fitting time."

67

WE HAD THE CORNER OF A Pullman car to ourselves that evening as we whirled back to London, and I fancy that the journey was a short one to Colonel Ross as well as to myself, as we listened to our companion's narrative.

"I confess," said Holmes, "that I went to Devonshire with the conviction that Fitzroy Simpson was the true culprit, although the evidence against him was by no means complete. It was while I was in the carriage, just as we reached the trainer's house, that the immense significance of the curried mutton occurred to me. You may remember that I was distrait, and remained sitting after you had all alighted. I was marveling in my own mind how I could possibly have overlooked so obvious a clue."

"Even now," said the colonel, "I cannot see how it helps us."

"It was the first link in my chain of reasoning. Powdered opium is by no means tasteless. Were it mixed with any ordinary dish, the eater would undoubtedly detect it, and would probably eat no more. A curry was exactly the medium which would disguise this taste. By no possible supposition could this stranger, Fitzroy Simpson, have caused curry to be served in the trainer's family that night, and it is surely too monstrous a coincidence to suppose that he happened to come along with powdered opium upon the very night when a dish happened to be served which would disguise the flavor. Therefore Simpson becomes eliminated from the case, and our attention centers upon Straker and his wife, the only two people who could have chosen curried mutton for supper that night. The opium was added after the dish was set aside for the stableboy, for the others had the same for supper with no ill effects. Which of them, then, had access to that dish without the maid seeing them?

"Before deciding that question I had grasped the significance of the silence of the dog, for one true inference invariably suggests others. The Simpson incident had shown me that a dog was kept in the stables, and yet, though someone had fetched out a horse, he had not barked enough to arouse the two lads in the loft. Obviously the visitor was someone the dog knew well.

"I was already convinced, or almost convinced, that John

Straker went down to the stables in the dead of the night and took out Silver Blaze. For what purpose? For a dishonest one, obviously, or why should he drug his own stableboy? And yet I was at a loss to know why. There have been cases before now where the trainers have made sure of great sums of money by laying against their own horses, through agents, and then prevented them from winning by fraud. Sometimes it is a pulling jockey. Sometimes it is some surer and subtler means. What was it here? I hoped that the contents of his pockets might help me to form a conclusion.

"And they did so. You cannot have forgotten the singular knife which was found in the dead man's hand, one which certainly no sane man would choose for a weapon. It was, as Dr. Watson told us, a knife which is used for the most delicate operations known in surgery. And it was to be used for a delicate operation that night. You must know, with your wide experience of turf matters, Colonel Ross, that it is possible to make a slight nick upon the tendons of a horse's ham, and to do it subcutaneously so as to leave absolutely no trace. A horse so treated would develop a slight lameness which would be put down to a strain in exercise or a touch of rheumatism, but never to foul play."

"Villain! Scoundrel!" cried the colonel.

"We have here the explanation of why Straker wished to take the horse out onto the moor. So spirited a creature would have certainly roused the soundest of sleepers when it felt the prick of the knife."

"I have been blind!" cried the colonel. "Of course, that was why he needed the candle, and struck the match."

"Undoubtedly. But in examining his belongings, I was fortunate enough to discover not only the method of the crime, but even its motives. As a man of the world, Colonel, you know that men do not carry other people's bills about in their pockets. We have most of us quite enough to do to settle our own. I at once concluded that Straker was leading a double life, and keeping a second establishment. The nature of the bill showed that there was a lady in the case, and one who had expensive tastes. Liberal as you are with your servants, one hardly expects that they can buy twenty-guinea walking dresses for their women. I questioned Mrs. Straker as to the dress without her knowing it, and having satisfied myself that it had never reached her, I made a note of the dressmaker's address, and felt that by calling there with Straker's photograph I could easily dispose of the mythical Darbyshire.

"From that time on all was plain. Straker had led out the horse to a hollow where his light would be invisible. Simpson, in his flight, had dropped his cravat, and Straker had picked it up with some idea, perhaps, that he might use it in securing the horse's leg. Once in the hollow he had got behind the horse, and had struck a light, but the creature, frightened at the sudden glare, and with the strange instinct of animals feeling that some mischief was intended, had lashed out, and the steel shoe had struck Straker full on the forehead. He had already, in spite of the rain, taken off his overcoat in order to do his delicate task, and so, as he fell, his knife gashed his thigh."

"Wonderful!" cried the colonel. "You might have been there."

"My final shot was, I confess, a very long one. It struck me that so astute a man as Straker would not undertake this delicate tendon-nicking without a little practice. What could he practice on? My eyes fell upon the sheep, and I asked a question which, rather to my surprise, showed that my surmise was correct.

"When I returned to London I called upon the dressmaker, who recognized Straker as an excellent customer of the name of Darbyshire, who had a dashing wife, with a partiality for expensive dresses. I have no doubt that this woman had plunged him over head and ears in debt, and so led him into this miserable plot."

"You have explained all but one thing," cried the colonel. "Where was the horse?"

"Ah, it bolted, and was cared for by one of your neighbors. We must have an amnesty in that direction, I think. This is Clapham Junction, if I am not mistaken, and we shall be in Victoria in less than ten minutes. If you care to smoke a cigar in our rooms, Colonel, I shall be happy to give you any other details which might interest you."

The Adventure of the Speckled Band

It was early in April, the year 1883, that I woke one morning to find Sherlock Holmes standing, fully dressed, by the side of my bed. The clock on the mantelpiece showed me that it was only a quarter past seven, and I blinked up at him in some surprise.

"Very sorry to wake you up, Watson," said he, "but it's the common lot this morning. Mrs. Hudson has been waked up, she retorted upon me, and I on you."

"What is it, then? A fire?"

"No, a client. A young lady has arrived in a considerable state of excitement, who insists upon seeing me. She is waiting now in the sitting room, and should it prove to be an interesting case, you would, I am sure, wish to follow it from the outset."

"My dear fellow, I would not miss it for anything." I threw on my clothes, and was ready in a few minutes to accompany my friend down to the sitting room. A lady dressed in black and heavily veiled, who had been sitting in the window, rose as we entered.

"Good morning, madam," said Holmes cheerily. "My name is Sherlock Holmes. This is my friend and associate, Dr. Watson, before whom you can speak as freely as before myself. Ha, I am glad to see that Mrs. Hudson has had the good sense to light the fire. Pray draw up to it, for I observe that you are shivering."

"It is not cold which makes me shiver, Mr. Holmes," said the woman in a low voice, changing her seat as requested. "It is terror." She raised her veil as she spoke, and we could see that she was indeed in a pitiable state of agitation, her face all drawn, with restless, frightened eyes. Her features and figure were those of a woman of thirty, but her hair was shot with premature gray, and her expression was weary and haggard.

"You must not fear," said Holmes soothingly, bending forward and patting her forearm. "We shall soon set matters right, I have no doubt. You have come in by train this morning, I see."

"You know me, then?"

"No, but I observe the second half of a return ticket in the palm of your left glove. You must have started early, and yet you had a good drive in a dogcart, along heavy roads, before you reached the station."

The lady stared in bewilderment at my companion.

"There is no mystery, my dear madam," said he, smiling. "The left arm of your jacket is spattered with mud, and the marks are perfectly fresh. Only a dogcart throws up mud in that way, and then only when you sit on the left-hand side of the driver."

"You are perfectly correct," said she. "I started from home before six, reached Leatherhead at twenty past, and came in by the first train to Waterloo. Oh, sir, I can stand this strain no longer. Do you not think you could throw a little light through the dense darkness which surrounds me? At present it is out of my power to reward you for your services, but in a month or two I shall be married, with the control of my own income, and then you shall not find me ungrateful."

"My profession is its reward, madam," said Holmes; "but you are at liberty to defray whatever expenses I may be put to, at the time which suits you best. And now I beg that you will lay before us everything that may help us in forming an opinion."

"Alas!" replied our visitor. "The very horror of my situation lies in the fact that my fears are so vague, and my suspicions depend entirely upon small points, which might seem trivial to another. But I have heard, Mr. Holmes, that you can see deeply into the manifold wickedness of the human heart."

"I am all attention, madam."

"My name is Helen Stoner, and I am living with my stepfather, who is the last survivor of one of the oldest Saxon families in England, the Roylotts of Stoke Moran, in Surrey."

Holmes nodded his head. "The name is familiar to me," said he.

"The family was at one time among the richest in England, and the estate was extensive. In the last century, however, four successive heirs were of a dissolute and wasteful disposition, and the family ruin was eventually completed by a gambler, in the days of the Regency. Nothing was left save a few acres of ground and the two-hundred-year-old house, which is itself crushed under a heavy mortgage. The last squire dragged out his existence there, living the horrible life of an aristocratic pauper; but his only son, my stepfather, seeing that he must adapt himself to the new conditions, obtained an advance from a relative, which enabled him to take a medical degree, and went out to Calcutta, where he established a large practice. In a fit of anger, however, caused by some robberies which had been perpetrated in the house, he beat his native butler to death, and narrowly escaped a capital sentence. As it was, he suffered a long term of imprisonment, and afterwards returned to England a morose and disappointed man.

"When Dr. Roylott was in India he married my mother, Mrs. Stoner, the young widow of Major General Stoner, of the Bengal Artillery. My sister Julia and I were twins, and we were only two years old at the time of my mother's remarriage. She had a considerable sum of money, not less than a thousand a year, and this she bequeathed to Dr. Roylott entirely whilst we resided with him, with a provision that a certain annual sum should be allowed to each of us in the event of our marriage. Shortly after our return to England, eight years ago, my mother died. Dr. Roylott then abandoned his attempts to establish a practice in London, and took us to live with him in the ancestral house at Stoke Moran. The money which my mother had left was enough for our wants, and there seemed no obstacle to our happiness.

"But a terrible change came over our stepfather about this time. He shut himself up in his house, and seldom came out save to indulge in ferocious quarrels with whoever might cross his path. Violence of temper approaching to mania has been hereditary in the men of the family, and in my stepfather's case it had, I believe, been intensified by his long residence in the tropics. A series of disgraceful brawls took place, two of which ended in the police court, until at last he became the terror of the village, and the folks

73

would fly at his approach, for he is a man of immense strength, and absolutely uncontrollable in his anger.

"He had no friends at all save the wandering gypsies, and he would give these vagabonds leave to encamp upon the few acres of bramble-covered land which represent the family estate, and would accept in return the hospitality of their tents, sometimes for weeks on end. He has a passion also for Indian animals, which are sent over to him by a correspondent, and he has at this moment a cheetah and a baboon, which wander freely over his grounds, and are feared by the villagers almost as much as their master. You can imagine that my poor sister Julia and I had no great pleasure in our lives. She was but thirty at the time of her death, and yet her hair had already begun to whiten, even as mine has."

"Your sister is dead, then?"

"She died just two years ago, and it is of her death that I wish to speak to you. You can understand that, living the life which I have described, we were little likely to see anyone of our own age and position. However, my mother's sister, Miss Honoria West-phail, lives near Harrow, and we were occasionally allowed to pay her short visits. Julia went there at Christmas two years ago, and met there a half-pay major of marines, to whom she became engaged. My stepfather learned of the engagement when my sister returned, and offered no objection; but within a fortnight of the day which had been fixed for the wedding, the terrible event occurred which has deprived me of my only companion."

Holmes had been leaning back in his chair with his eyes closed, his head sunk in a cushion, but he half opened his lids now, and glanced at his visitor. "Pray be precise as to details," said he.

"It is easy for me to be so, for every event of that dreadful time is seared into my memory. Only one wing of the manor house is now inhabited. The bedrooms in this wing are on the ground floor, the sitting rooms being in the central block of the buildings. Of these bedrooms, the first is Dr. Roylott's, the second my sister's, and the third my own. There is no communication between them, but they all open out into the same corridor. The windows of the three rooms open out upon the lawn.

THE ADVENTURE OF THE SPECKLED BAND

SILVER BLAZE

THE ADVENTURE OF THE DANCING MEN

THE ADVENTURE OF THE COPPER BEECHES

THE REIGATE SQUIRES

THE ADVENTURE OF THE BLUE CARBUNCLE

THE MAN WITH THE TWISTED LIP

THE RED-HEADED LEAGUE

"That fatal night Dr. Roylott had gone to his room early, though we knew that he had not retired to rest, for my sister was troubled by the smell of the strong Indian cigars which it was his custom to smoke. She left her room, therefore, and came into mine, where she sat for some time, chatting about her approaching wedding. At eleven o'clock she rose to leave me, but she paused at the door and looked back. 'Tell me, Helen,' she said, 'have you ever heard any-one whistle in the dead of the night?'

"'Never,' said I. 'But why?'

"'Because during the last few nights I have always, about three in the morning, heard a low clear whistle. I am a light sleeper, and it has awakened me. I cannot tell where it came from—perhaps from the next room, perhaps from the lawn.'

"'It must be those wretched gypsies in the plantation,' I said.

"'Very likely. And yet if it were on the lawn I wonder that you did not hear it also.'

"'Ah, but I sleep more heavily than you.'

"'Well, it is of no great consequence.' She smiled, closed my door, and a few moments later I heard her key turn in the lock."

"Indeed," said Holmes. "Was it your custom always to lock yourselves in at night?"

"Always. We had no feeling of security unless our doors were locked."

"Pray proceed with your statement."

"I could not sleep that night. A vague feeling of impending mis-fortune impressed me. My sister and I, you will recollect, were twins, and you know how subtle are the links which bind two souls so closely allied. It was a wild night. The wind was howling out-side, and the rain was beating and splashing against the windows. Suddenly, amidst all the hubbub of the gale, there burst forth the scream of a terrified woman. I knew that it was my sister's voice. I sprang from my bed, wrapped a shawl round me, and rushed into the corridor. As I opened my door I seemed to hear a low whistle, such as my sister described, and a few moments later a clanging sound, as if a mass of metal had fallen.

"As I ran down the passage my sister's door was unlocked, and

75

revolved slowly upon its hinges. I stared at it horror-stricken. By the light of the corridor lamp I saw my sister appear at the opening, her face blanched with terror, her hands groping for help, her whole figure swaying to and fro. I ran to her and threw my arms round her, but at that moment her knees gave way and she fell to the ground, writhing as if in terrible pain, her limbs dreadfully convulsed. As I bent over her she shrieked out in a voice which I shall never forget, 'O, my God! Helen! It was the band! The speckled band!' There was something else which she would fain have said, and she stabbed with her finger in the direction of the doctor's room, but a fresh convulsion seized her and choked her words. I rushed out, calling for my stepfather, and I met him hastening from his room in his dressing gown. When he reached my sister's side she was unconscious, and though he poured brandy down her throat, and sent for medical aid from the village, all efforts were in vain, for she slowly sank and died without recovering consciousness."

"One moment," said Holmes; "was your sister dressed?"

"No, she was in her nightdress. In her right hand was found the charred stump of a match, and in her left a matchbox."

"Showing that she had struck a light and looked about her when the alarm took place. That is important. And what conclusions did the coroner come to?"

"He investigated the case with great care, for Dr. Roylott's conduct had long been notorious in the county, but he was unable to find any satisfactory cause of death. My evidence showed that the door had been fastened upon the inner side, and the windows were blocked by old-fashioned shutters with broad iron bars, which were secured every night. The walls were carefully sounded, and were shown to be quite solid all round, and the flooring was also thoroughly examined, with the same result. The chimney is wide, but is barred up by four large staples. It is certain, therefore, that my sister was quite alone when she met her end. Besides, there were no marks of any violence upon her."

"How about poison?"

"The doctors examined her for it, but without success."

"Were there gypsies in the plantation at the time?"

"Yes, there are nearly always some there."

"Ah, and what did you gather from this allusion to a band—a speckled band?"

"Sometimes I have thought that it was merely the wild talk of delirium, sometimes that it may have referred to the band of gypsies in the plantation. Perhaps the spotted handkerchiefs which so many of them wear over their heads might have suggested it to her."

Holmes shook his head like a man who is far from satisfied. "These are very deep waters," said he. "Pray go on."

"Two years have passed since then, and my life has been until lately lonelier than ever. A month ago, however, a dear friend, whom I have known for many years, did me the honor to ask my hand in marriage. His name is Percy Armitage, the second son of Mr. Armitage, of Crane Water, near Reading. My stepfather has offered no opposition, and we are to be married this spring. Two days ago some repairs were started in the west wing of the building, and my bedroom wall has been pierced, so that I have had to move into the chamber in which my sister died, and to sleep in the very bed in which she slept. Imagine, then, my terror when last night, as I lay awake thinking over her terrible fate, I suddenly heard the low whistle which had been the herald of her own death. I sprang up and lit the lamp, but nothing was to be seen in the room. I was too shaken to go to bed again, however, so I dressed, and as soon as it was daylight I slipped down, got a dogcart at the Crown Inn, and started for London to see you."

"You have done wisely," said my friend. "This is very deep business. There are a thousand details which I should desire to know before I decide upon our course of action. Yet we have not a moment to lose. If we were to come to Stoke Moran today, would it be possible for us to see these rooms without the knowledge of your stepfather?"

"As it happens, he spoke of coming into town today upon some most important business. It is probable that he will be away all day, and that there would be nothing to disturb you."

77

"Excellent. You are not averse to this trip, Watson?"

"By no means."

"Then you may expect us both early in the afternoon. What are you going to do yourself?"

"I have one or two things which I would wish to do now that I am in town. But I shall return by the twelve-o'clock train, so as to be there in time for your coming." The lady rose, dropped her thick black veil over her face, and glided from the room.

"And what do you think of it all, Watson?" asked Sherlock Holmes, leaning back in his chair.

"I cannot imagine. It seems to me to be a most dark and sinister business."

"Yet when you combine the ideas of whistles at night, the presence of a band of gypsies who are on intimate terms with this old doctor, the fact that the doctor has an interest in preventing his stepdaughter's marriage, the dying allusion to a band, and finally, the fact that Miss Stoner heard a metallic clang, which might have been caused by one of those metal bars which secured the shutters falling back into its place, there is good ground to think that the mystery may be cleared along these lines. But what, in the name of the devil!"

The ejaculation had been drawn from my companion by the fact that our door had been suddenly dashed open, and that a huge man framed himself in the aperture. His costume was a peculiar mixture of the professional and of the agricultural, having a black top hat, a long frock coat, and a pair of high gaiters, with a hunting crop swinging in his hand. So tall was he that his hat brushed the crossbar of the doorway, and his breadth seemed to span it across from side to side. A large face, seared with a thousand wrinkles, burned yellow with the sun, and marked with every evil passion, was turned from one to the other of us, while his deep-set eyes and the high, thin, fleshless nose, gave him somewhat the resemblance to a fierce old bird of prey.

"Which of you is Holmes?" asked this apparition.

"My name, sir, but you have the advantage of me," said my companion quietly.

"I am Dr. Grimesby Roylott, of Stoke Moran."

"Indeed, Doctor," said Holmes blandly. "Pray take a seat."

"I will do nothing of the kind. My stepdaughter has been here. I have traced her. What has she been saying to you?"

"It is a little cold for the time of the year," said Holmes.

"What has she been saying to you?" screamed the old man.

"But I have heard that the crocuses promise well," continued my companion imperturbably.

"Ha! You put me off, do you?" said our new visitor, taking a step forward, and shaking his hunting crop. "I know you, you scoundrel! I have heard of you before. You are Holmes the meddler, the Scotland Yard jack-in-office."

Holmes chuckled. "Your conversation is most entertaining. When you go out close the door, for there is a decided draft."

"I will go when I have had my say. Don't you dare to meddle with my affairs. I am a dangerous man to fall foul of! See here." He stepped swiftly forward, seized the poker, and bent it into a curve with his huge brown hands. "See that you keep yourself out of my grip," he snarled, and hurling the twisted poker into the fireplace, he strode out of the room.

"He seems a very amiable person," said Holmes, laughing. "I am not quite so bulky, but if he had remained I might have shown him that my grip was not much more feeble than his own." As he spoke he picked up the steel poker, and with a sudden effort straightened it out again.

"Fancy his having the insolence to confound me with the official detective force! This incident gives zest to our investigation, however, and I only trust that our little friend will not suffer from her imprudence in allowing this brute to trace her. Now we shall order breakfast, and then I shall go to Doctors' Commons, where I hope to get some data which may be helpful to us."

IT WAS NEARLY ONE O'CLOCK when Sherlock Holmes returned from his excursion. "I have seen the will of the deceased wife," said he. "The total income, which at the time of the wife's death was little short of eleven hundred pounds, is now through the fall in agricultural prices not more than seven hundred fifty pounds. In case of marriage, each daughter can claim an income of two hundred fifty pounds. It is evident, therefore, that if both girls had married, this beauty would have had a mere pittance, while even one of them would cripple him to a serious extent. My morning's work has proved that he has the very strongest motives for standing in the way of anything of the sort. And now, Watson, this is too serious for dawdling, especially as the old man is aware that we are interesting ourselves in his affairs, so if you are ready we shall call a cab and drive to Waterloo. I should be very much obliged if you would slip your revolver into your pocket. That and a toothbrush are, I think, all that you need."

At Waterloo we caught a train for Leatherhead, where we hired a trap at the station inn, and drove for four or five miles through the lovely Surrey lanes. It was a perfect spring day, with a bright sun and a few fleecy clouds in the heavens, and the air was full of the pleasant smell of the moist earth. To me at least there was a strange contrast between the sweet promise of the spring and this sinister quest upon which we were engaged. My companion sat with his arms folded, his hat pulled down over his eyes, and his chin sunk upon his breast, buried in thought.

Suddenly, however, he started, tapped me on the shoulder, and pointed over the meadows. "Look there!" said he. A heavily timbered park stretched up in a gentle slope, thickening into a grove at the highest point. From amidst the branches there jutted the gray stables of an old mansion. "Stoke Moran?" said he.

"Yes, sir; and there's the village," said the driver, pointing to a cluster of roofs some distance to the left; "but if you want to get to the house, you'll find it shorter to go over this stile, and so by the footpath over the fields. There it is, where the lady is walking."

"And the lady, I fancy, is Miss Stoner," observed Holmes, shading his eyes. "Yes, I think we had better do as you suggest."

We got off, paid our fare, and the trap rattled back on its way to Leatherhead. We climbed the stile.

"Good afternoon, Miss Stoner," said Holmes. "You see that we have been as good as our word."

Our client's face spoke her joy. "I have been waiting so eagerly for you," she cried, shaking hands with us warmly.

"We haye had the pleasure of making Dr. Roylott's acquaintance," said Holmes, and in a few words he sketched out what had occurred. Miss Stoner turned white as she listened.

"Good heavens!" she cried. "He has followed me, then. He is so cunning. What will he say when he returns?"

"He must guard himself, for he may find that there is someone more cunning than himself upon his track. Now, we must make the best use of our time, so kindly take us at once to the rooms which we are to examine."

The building was of gray, lichen-blotched stone, with a high central portion, and two curving wings, like the claws of a crab, thrown out on each side. In one of these wings the windows were broken, and blocked with wooden boards, while the roof was partly caved in, a picture of ruin. The central portion was in little better repair, but the right-hand block was comparatively modern, and the blinds in the windows, with the blue smoke curling up from the chimneys, showed that this was where the family resided. Some scaffolding had been erected against the end wall, and the stonework had been broken into, but there were no signs of any workmen. Holmes walked slowly up and down the ill-trimmed lawn, and examined the windows with deep attention.

"This, I take it, belongs to the room in which you used to sleep, the center one to your sister's, and the one next to the main building to Dr. Roylott's chamber?"

"Exactly so. But I am now sleeping in the middle one."

"Pending the alterations, as I understand. By the way, there does not seem to be any need for repairs at that end wall."

"There were none. I believe that it was an excuse to move me from my room."

"Ah! That is suggestive. Now, on the other side of this narrow wing runs the corridor from which these three rooms open. There are windows in it, of course?"

"Yes, but they are too narrow for anyone to pass through."

"As you both locked your doors at night, your rooms were

unapproachable from that side. Now, would you have the kindness to go into your room, and to bar your shutters."

Miss Stoner did so, and Holmes endeavored in every way to force the shutter open, but without success. There was no slit through which a knife could be passed to raise the bar. Then with his lens he tested the hinges, but they were of solid iron, built firmly into the massive masonry. "Hum!" said he, scratching his chin in some perplexity. "My theory certainly presents some difficulties. No one could pass these shutters if they were bolted. Well, we shall see if the inside throws any light upon the matter."

A small side door led into the whitewashed corridor from which the three bedrooms opened. We passed at once to the chamber in which Miss Stoner was now sleeping, and in which her sister had met her fate. It was a homely little room, with a low ceiling and a gaping fireplace, after the fashion of old country houses. A brown chest of drawers stood in one corner, a narrow bed in another, and a narrow table on the left side of the window. These articles, with two small wickerwork chairs, made up all the furniture in the room, save for a square of Wilton carpet in the center. The paneling of the walls was brown, worm-eaten oak, so old and discolored that it may have dated from the original building of the house. Holmes drew one of the chairs into a corner and sat silent, while his eyes traveled round and round and up and down, taking in every detail.

"Where does that bell communicate with?" he asked at last, pointing to a thick bell rope which hung down beside the bed, the tassel actually lying upon the pillow.

"It goes to the housekeeper's room."

"It looks newer than the other things."

"Yes, it was only put there a couple of years ago."

"Your sister asked for it, I suppose?"

"No, I never heard of her using it. We used always to get what we wanted for ourselves."

Holmes then threw himself down upon his face with his lens in his hand, and crawled swiftly backwards and forwards, examining minutely the cracks between the boards. He did the same with the woodwork with which the chamber was paneled. Then he walked over to the bed and spent some time in staring at it, and in running his eye up and down the wall. Finally he took the bell rope in his hand and gave it a brisk tug. "Why, it's a dummy," said he. "It is not even attached to a wire. This is very interesting.

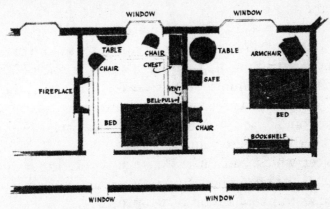

You can see now that it is fastened to a hook just above where the little opening of the ventilator is."

"How very absurd! I never noticed that before."

"Very strange!" muttered Holmes, pulling at the rope. "There are one or two very singular points about this room. For example, what a fool a builder must be to open a ventilator into another room, when, with the same trouble, he might have communicated with the outside air!"

"That is also quite modern," said the lady.

"Done about the same time as the bell rope," said Holmes.

"Yes, there were several changes carried out about that time."

"They seem to have been of a most interesting character— dummy bell ropes, and ventilators which do not ventilate. With your permission, Miss Stoner, we shall now carry our researches into the inner apartment."

Dr. Grimesby Roylott's chamber was larger than that of his stepdaughter, but was as plainly furnished. A camp bed, a small wooden shelf full of books, mostly of a technical character, an armchair beside the bed, a plain wooden chair against the wall, a round table, and a large iron safe were the principal things which met the eye. Holmes walked slowly round and examined each and all of them with the keenest interest.

"Is there a cat in here?" he asked, tapping the safe.

"What a strange idea!"

"Well, look at this!" He took up a small saucer of milk which stood on the top of the safe.

"We don't keep a cat. But there are a cheetah and a baboon."

"Well, a cheetah is just a big cat, and yet a saucer of milk does not go far in satisfying it, I daresay. There is one point which I should wish to determine." He squatted in front of the wooden chair, and examined its seat with great attention.

"Thank you. That is quite settled," said he, rising. "Hullo! Here is something interesting!"

The object which had caught his eye was a dog lash hung on one corner of the bed. The lash, however, was curled upon itself, and tied so as to make a loop of whipcord.

"What do you make of that, Watson?"

"It's a common enough lash. But why should it be tied?"

"That is not quite so common, is it? Ah, me! It's a wicked world, and when a clever man turns his brain to crime it is the worst of all. I think that I have seen enough now, Miss Stoner, and, with your permission, we shall walk out upon the lawn."

I had never seen my friend's face so grim, or his brow so dark, as it was when we turned from the scene of this investigation. We had walked several times up and down the lawn, neither Miss Stoner nor myself liking to break in upon his thoughts before he roused himself from his reverie. "It is essential, Miss Stoner," said he, "that you should follow my advice in every respect. Your life may depend upon your compliance."

"I assure you that I am in your hands."

"In the first place, my friend and I must spend the night in your room."

Both Miss Stoner and I gazed at him in astonishment.

"Let me explain. I believe that that is the village inn over there?"

"Yes, that is the Crown."

"Very good. Your windows would be visible from there?"

"Certainly."

"You must confine yourself to your room, on pretense of a headache, when your stepfather comes back. Then when you hear him retire for the night, you must open the shutters of your window, undo the hasp, put your lamp there as a signal to us, and then withdraw into the room which you used to occupy. The rest you will leave in our hands. We shall spend the night in your room, and we shall investigate the cause of this noise which has disturbed you."

"I believe, Mr. Holmes, that you have already made up your mind," said Miss Stoner, laying her hand upon his sleeve.

"Perhaps I have."

"Then for pity's sake tell me what caused my sister's death."

"I should prefer to have clearer proofs before I speak. And now, Miss Stoner, we must leave you, for if Dr. Roylott returned and saw us, our journey would be in vain. Good-by, and be brave, for if you will do what I have told you, you may rest assured that we shall soon drive away the dangers that threaten you."

Sherlock Holmes and I had no difficulty in engaging a bedroom and sitting room at the Crown Inn. They were on the upper floor, and from our window we could command a view of the avenue gate, and of the inhabited wing of Stoke Moran manor house. At dusk we saw Dr. Grimesby Roylott drive past, his huge form looming up beside the little figure of the lad who drove him. The boy had some slight difficulty in undoing the heavy iron gates, and we heard the hoarse roar of the doctor's voice, and saw the fury with which he shook his clenched fists at him. The trap drove on, and a few minutes later we saw a sudden light spring up among the trees as the lamp was lit in one of the sitting rooms.

"Do you know, Watson," said Holmes, as we sat together in the gathering darkness, "I have really some scruples as to taking you tonight. There is a distinct element of danger."

"If I can be of assistance I shall certainly come."

"It is very kind of you."

"You speak of danger. You have evidently seen more in those rooms than was visible to me."

"No, but I fancy that I may have deduced a little more. You saw the ventilator?"

"Yes, but I do not think that it is such a very unusual thing to have a small opening between two rooms."

"I knew before we came here that we should find a ventilator."

"My dear Holmes!"

"Oh, yes, I did. You remember in her statement Miss Stoner said that her sister could smell Dr. Roylott's cigar. Now, of course that suggests at once that there must be a communication between the two rooms. It could only be a small one, or it would have been remarked upon at the coroner's inquiry. I deduced a ventilator. Then there is the curious coincidence of dates. A ventilator is made, a cord is hung, and a lady who sleeps in the bed dies. Did you observe anything very peculiar about that bed?"

"No."

"It was clamped to the floor so the lady could not move it. The bed must always be in the same relative position to the ventilator and to the rope—for so we may call it, since it was clearly never meant for a bellpull."

"Holmes," I cried, "I see dimly what you are hitting at. We are only just in time to prevent some subtle and horrible crime."

"When a doctor does go wrong he is the first of criminals. He has nerve and he has knowledge. I think, Watson, that we shall have horrors enough before the night is over; so for goodness' sake let us have a quiet pipe, and turn our minds for a few hours to something more cheerful."

ABOUT NINE O'CLOCK THE LIGHT among the trees was extinguished, and all was dark in the direction of the manor house. Two hours passed slowly away, and then, suddenly, just at the stroke of eleven, a single bright light shone out right in front of us.

"That is our signal," said Holmes, springing to his feet. "It comes from the middle window."

As we passed out he exchanged a few words with the landlord, explaining that we were going on a late visit to an acquaintance, and that it was possible that we might spend the night there. A moment later we were out on the dark road, a chill wind blowing in our faces, and one yellow light twinkling in front of us through the gloom to guide us on our somber errand. There was little difficulty in entering the grounds, for unrepaired breaches gaped in the old park wall. Making our way among the trees, we reached the lawn, crossed it, and were about to enter through the window, when out from a clump of laurel bushes there darted what seemed to be a hideous and distorted child, who ran swiftly across the lawn into the darkness.

"My God!" I whispered. "Did you see it?"

Holmes was for the moment as startled as I. His hand closed like a vise upon my wrist in his agitation. Then he broke into a low laugh, and put his lips to my ear. "It is a nice household," he murmured. "That is the baboon."

I had forgotten the strange pets which the doctor affected. There was a cheetah, too; perhaps we might find it upon our shoulders at any moment. I confess that I felt easier in my mind when, after following Holmes's example and slipping off my shoes, I found myself inside the bedroom. My companion noiselessly closed the shutters, moved the lamp onto the table, and cast his eyes round the room. All was as we had seen it in the daytime. Then creeping up to me and making a trumpet of his hand, he whispered into my ear, "The least sound would be fatal to our plans."

I nodded to show that I had heard.

"We must sit without a light. He would see it through the ventilator. Do not go to sleep; your very life may depend upon it. Have your pistol ready in case we should need it. I will sit on the side of the bed, and you in that chair."

I took out my revolver and laid it on the corner of the table.

Holmes had brought a long thin cane, and this he placed upon the bed beside him. By it he laid the box of matches and the stump of a candle. Then he turned down the lamp.

How shall I ever forget that dreadful vigil? I could not hear a sound, not even the drawing of a breath, and yet I knew that my companion sat open-eyed, within a few feet of me, in the same state of nervous tension in which I was myself. We waited in absolute darkness. From outside came the occasional cry of a night bird, and once at our very window a long-drawn, catlike whine, which told us that the cheetah was indeed at liberty. Far away we could hear the deep tones of the parish clock, which boomed out every quarter of an hour. How long they seemed, those quarters! Twelve o'clock, and one, and two, and three, and still we sat waiting silently for whatever might befall.

Suddenly there was the momentary gleam of a light up in the direction of the ventilator. It vanished immediately, but was succeeded by a strong smell of burning oil and heated metal. Someone in the next room had lit a dark lantern. I heard a gentle sound of movement, and then all was silent once more, though the smell grew stronger. For half an hour I sat with straining ears. Then another sound became audible—a very gentle, soothing sound, like that of a small jet of steam escaping continually from a kettle. The instant that we heard it, Holmes sprang from the bed, struck a match, and lashed furiously with his cane at the bellpull.

"You see it, Watson?" he yelled. "You see it?"

But I saw nothing. At the moment when Holmes struck the light I heard a low, clear whistle, but the sudden glare flashing into my weary eyes made it impossible for me to tell what it was at which my friend lashed so savagely. I could, however, see that his face was deadly pale, and filled with horror and loathing.

He had ceased to strike, and was gazing up at the ventilator, when suddenly there broke from the silence of the night the most horrible cry to which I have ever listened. It swelled up louder and louder, a hoarse yell of pain and fear and anger all mingled in the one dreadful shriek. They say that away down in the village, and even in the distant parsonage, that cry raised the sleepers from their beds. It struck cold to our hearts, and I stood gazing at Holmes, and he at me, until the last echoes of it had died away.

"What can it mean?" I gasped.

"It means that it is all over," Holmes answered. "And perhaps, after all, it is for the best. Take your pistol, and we shall enter Dr. Roylott's room."

With a grave face he lit the lamp, and led the way down the corridor. Twice he struck at the chamber door without any reply from within. Then he turned the handle and entered, I at his heels with the cocked pistol in my hand.

It was a singular sight which met our eyes. On the table stood a dark lantern with the shutter half open, throwing a brilliant beam of light upon the iron safe, the door of which was ajar. Beside this table, on the wooden chair, sat Dr. Grimesby Roylott, clad in a long gray dressing gown, his bare ankles protruding beneath, and his feet thrust into red heelless Turkish slippers. Across his lap lay the short stock with the long lash which we had noticed during the day. His chin was cocked upwards, and his eyes were fixed in a dreadful, rigid stare at the corner of the ceiling. A peculiar yellow band, with brownish speckles, seemed to be bound tightly round his head.

"The band! The speckled band!" whispered Holmes.

I took a step forward. In an instant the doctor's strange head-gear began to move, and there reared itself from among his hair the squat diamond-shaped head and puffed neck of a loathsome serpent.

"It is a swamp adder!" cried Holmes. "The deadliest snake in India. He has died within ten seconds of being bitten. Violence does, in truth, recoil upon the violent. Let us thrust this creature back into its den, and we can then remove Miss Stoner to some place of shelter, and let the police know what has happened."

As he spoke he drew the dog whip swiftly from the dead man's lap, and throwing the noose round the reptile's neck, he pulled it from its horrid perch, and, carrying it at arm's length, threw it into the iron safe, which he closed upon it.

SUCH WAS THE DEATH of Dr. Grimesby Roylott, of Stoke Moran. It is not necessary that I should prolong my narrative by telling how we broke the sad news to the terrified girl, how we conveyed her by the morning train to the care of her good aunt at Harrow, of how the slow process of official inquiry came to the conclusion that the doctor met his fate while indiscreetly playing with a dangerous pet. The little which I had yet to learn of the case was told me by Sherlock Holmes as we traveled back the next day.

"I had," said he, "come to an entirely erroneous conclusion, which shows, my dear Watson, how dangerous it is to reason from insufficient data. The presence of the gypsies, and the word 'band,' which was used by the poor girl, no doubt, to explain the appearance which she had caught a horrid glimpse of by the light of her match, were sufficient to put me upon an entirely wrong scent. I can only claim the merit that I instantly reconsidered my position when it became clear to me that whatever danger threatened an occupant of the room could not come either from the window or the door. My attention was speedily drawn to this ventilator, and to the bell rope which hung down to the bed. The discovery that this was a dummy bellpull, and that the bed was clamped to the floor, gave rise to the suspicion that the rope was there as a bridge for something passing through the hole, and coming to the bed. The idea of a snake instantly occurred to me, and when I coupled it with my knowledge that the doctor was furnished with a supply of creatures from India, I felt that I was on the right track. The idea of using a form of poison which could not possibly be discovered by any chemical test was just such a one as would occur to a clever and ruthless man who had had an Eastern training. The rapidity with which such a poison would take effect would also, from his point of view, be an advantage. It would be a sharp-eyed coroner indeed who could distinguish the two little dark punctures which would show where the poison fangs had done their work.

"Then I thought of the whistle. Of course Dr. Roylott must recall the snake before morning light revealed it to the victim. He had trained it, probably by the use of the milk which we saw, to return to him when summoned. He would put it through the ventilator at the hour that he thought best, with the certainty that it would crawl down the rope, and land on the bed. It might or might not bite the occupant; perhaps she might escape every night for a week, but sooner or later she must fall a victim.

"I had come to these conclusions before ever I had entered his room. An inspection of his chair showed me that he had been in the habit of standing on it, which would be necessary in order that he should reach the ventilator. The sight of the safe, the saucer of milk, and the loop of whipcord were enough to dispel any doubts which may have remained. The metallic clang heard by Miss Stoner was obviously caused by her stepfather closing the door of his safe upon its terrible occupant. Having once made up my mind, you know the steps which I took to put the matter to the proof. I heard the creature hiss, as I have no doubt you did also, and I instantly lit the light and attacked it."

"With the result of driving it through the ventilator."

"And also with the result of causing it to turn upon its master at the other side. Some of the blows of my cane came home, and roused its snakish temper, so that it flew upon the first person it saw. In this way I am no doubt indirectly responsible for Dr. Grimesby Roylott's death, and I cannot say that it is likely to weigh very heavily upon my conscience."

The Reigate Squires

ON REFERRING TO MY NOTES, I see that it was on the fourteenth of April, 1887, that I received a telegram from Lyons which informed me that Holmes was lying ill in the Hotel Dulong. Within twenty-four hours I was in his sickroom, and was relieved to find that there was nothing formidable in his symptoms. His iron constitution, however, had broken down under the strain of an investigation which had extended over two months, during which period he had never worked less than fifteen hours a day; and despite the triumphant issue of his labors, I found him a prey to the blackest depression.

Three days later we were back in Baker Street together, but it was evident that my friend would be much the better for a change, and the thought of a week of springtime in the country was full of attractions to me also. My old friend Colonel Hayter, who had come under my professional care in Afghanistan, had now taken a house near Reigate, in Surrey, and had frequently asked me to come down to him upon a visit. On the last occasion he had remarked that he would be glad to extend his hospitality to my friend also. Holmes fell in with my plans, and a week after our return from Lyons, we were under the colonel's roof.

On the evening of our arrival we were sitting in the colonel's gun room after dinner, Holmes stretched upon the sofa, while Hayter and I looked over his little armory of firearms.

"By the way," said the colonel suddenly, "I'll take one of these pistols upstairs with me in case we have an alarm."

"An alarm!" said I.

"Yes, we've had a scare in this part lately. Old Acton, who is one of our county magnates, had his house broken into last Monday. No great damage done, but the fellows are still at large."

"No clue?" asked Holmes, cocking his eye at the colonel.

"None as yet. But the affair is a petty one, too small for your attention, Mr. Holmes."

Holmes waved away the compliment, though his smile showed that it had pleased him. "Was there any feature of interest?"

"I fancy not. The thieves got very little for their pains. The whole library was turned upside down, drawers burst open and cupboards ransacked, with the result that an odd volume of Pope's *Homer*, two plated candlesticks, an ivory letterweight, a small oak barometer, and a ball of twine are all that have vanished. The fellows evidently grabbed hold of anything they could get."

Holmes grunted from the sofa. "The county police ought to make something of that," said he. "Why, it is surely obvious that—"

But I held up a warning finger. "You are here for a rest, my dear fellow. For heaven's sake, don't get started on a new problem when your nerves are all in shreds."

Holmes shrugged his shoulders with a glance of comic resignation towards the colonel, and the talk drifted away into less dangerous channels.

It was destined, however, that all my professional caution should be wasted, for next morning, when we were at breakfast, the colonel's butler rushed in with all his propriety shaken out of him. "Have you heard the news, sir?" he gasped. "At the Cunninghams', sir!"

"Burglary?" cried the colonel, with his coffee cup in midair.

"Murder!"

The colonel whistled. "By Jove!" said he. "Who's killed, then?"

"William, the coachman, sir. The burglar shot him and got clean away. He'd just broke in at the kitchen door, somewhere about twelve, when William came on him and met his end in saving his master's property."

"Ah, then, we'll step over presently," said the colonel, coolly settling down to his breakfast again. "It's a bad business," he added, when the butler had gone. "Old Cunningham is our leading squire about here, and a very decent fellow, too. He'll be cut up over this, for the man has been in his service for years, and was a good servant. It's evidently the same villains who broke into Acton's."

"And stole that singular collection?" said Holmes thoughtfully.

"Precisely."

"Hum! This is a little curious, is it not? A gang of burglars acting in the country might be expected to vary the scene of their operations, and not to crack two cribs in the same district within a few days. When you spoke last night of taking precautions, it passed through my mind that this was probably the last parish in England to which the thief or thieves would be likely to turn their attention; which shows that I have still much to learn."

"I fancy it's some local practitioner," said the colonel. "In that case, of course, Acton's and Cunningham's are just the places he would go for, since they are far the largest about here."

"And richest?"

"Well, they ought to be; but they've had a lawsuit for some years which has sucked the blood out of both of them, I fancy. Old Acton has some claim on half Cunningham's estate, and the lawyers have been at it with both hands."

"If it's a local villain, there should not be much difficulty in running him down," said Holmes with a yawn. "All right, Watson, I don't intend to meddle."

"Inspector Forrester, sir," said the butler, opening the door.

The official, a smart, keen-faced young fellow, stepped into the room. "Good morning, Colonel," said he. "I hope I don't intrude, but we hear that Mr. Holmes, of Baker Street, is here."

The colonel waved his hand towards my friend, and the inspector bowed. "We thought you might care to step across, Mr. Holmes."

"The Fates are against you, Watson," said he, laughing. "We were chatting about the matter when you came in, Inspector. Perhaps you can let us have a few details." As he leaned back in his chair in the familiar attitude, I knew that the case was hopeless.

"We had no clue in the Acton affair. But here we have plenty to go on. The man was seen."

"Ah!"

"Yes, sir. But he was off like a deer after the shot that killed poor

William Kirwan was fired. Mr. Cunningham saw him from the bedroom window, and his son, Mr. Alec Cunningham, saw him from the back passage. It was a quarter to twelve when the alarm broke out. Mr. Cunningham had just got into bed, and Mister Alec was smoking a pipe in his dressing room. They both heard William calling for help, and Mister Alec ran down to see what was the matter. The back door was open, and as he came to the foot of the stairs he saw two men wrestling together outside. One of them fired a shot, the other dropped, and the murderer rushed across the garden and over the hedge. Mr. Cunningham, looking out of his bedroom window, saw the fellow as he gained the road, but lost sight of him at once. Mister Alec stopped to see if he could help the dying man, and so the villain got away. Beyond the fact that he was a middle-sized man, and dressed in some dark stuff, we have no personal clue, but we are making energetic inquiries."

"What was this William doing there? Did he say anything before he died?"

"Not a word. He lives at the lodge with his mother, and as he was a very faithful fellow, we imagine that he walked up to the house with the intention of seeing that all was right there. Of course, this Acton business has put everyone on his guard. The robber must have just burst open the door—the lock has been forced—when William came upon him. We found one important piece of evidence. Look at this!"

He took a small piece of torn paper from a notebook and spread it out upon his knee. "This was found between the finger and thumb of the dead man. It appears to be a fragment torn from a larger sheet. You will observe that the hour mentioned upon it is the very time at which the poor fellow met his fate. You see that his murderer might have torn the rest of the sheet from him or he might have taken this fragment from the murderer. It reads almost as though it was an appointment."

Holmes took up the scrap of paper.

"Presuming that it is an appointment," continued the inspector, "it is, of course, a conceivable theory that this William Kirwan, although he had the reputation of being an honest man, may have been in league with the thief. He may have met him there, may even have helped him to break in the door, and then they may have fallen out between themselves."

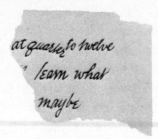

at quarter to twelve
' learn what
maybe

"This writing is of extraordinary interest," said Holmes, who had been examining it with intense concentration, "and your supposition is ingenious. These are much deeper waters than I had thought." He sank his head upon his hands, while the inspector smiled at the effect which his case had had upon the famous London specialist.

Holmes remained for some minutes in the deepest thought. When he raised his face I was surprised to see that his cheek was tinged with color, and his eyes as bright as before his illness. He sprang to his feet with all his old energy. "I'll tell you what!" said he. "I should like to have a quiet glance into the details of this case. There is something in it which fascinates me extremely. If you will permit me, Colonel, I will leave my friend Watson and you, and I will step round with the inspector to test the truth of one or two little fancies of mine."

An hour and a half had elapsed before the inspector returned alone. "Mr. Holmes is outside," said he. "He wants us all four to go up to Mr. Cunningham's house together. Between ourselves, I think Mr. Holmes has not quite got over his illness yet. He's behaving very queerly, and he is very much excited."

"I don't think you need alarm yourself," said I. "I have usually found that there was method in his madness."

"Some folk might say there was madness in his method," muttered the inspector. "We had best go out, if you are ready."

We found Holmes pacing up and down in the field, his chin sunk upon his breast, and his hands thrust into his trouser pockets. "The matter grows in interest," said he. "Watson, your country trip has been a distinct success. I have had a charming morning. The inspector and I have made quite a little reconnaissance together. I'll tell you what we did as we walk. First of all we saw the body of this unfortunate man. He certainly died from a revolver wound, as reported."

"Had you doubted it, then?"

"Oh, it is as well to test everything. Our inspection was not wasted. We then interviewed Mr. Cunningham and his son, who were able to point out the exact spot where the murderer had broken through the hedge in his flight. That was of great interest."

"Naturally."

"Then we saw this poor fellow's mother. We could get no information from her, however, as she is very old and deaf."

"And what is the result of your investigations?"

"The conviction that the crime is a very peculiar one. Perhaps our visit now may do something to make it less obscure. I think that we are both agreed, Inspector, that the fragment of paper in the dead man's hand, bearing, as it does, the very hour of his death written upon it, is of extreme importance. Whoever wrote that note was the man who brought William Kirwan out of his bed at that hour. But where is the rest of that sheet of paper?"

"I examined the ground carefully in the hope of finding it," said the inspector.

"It was torn out of the dead man's hand. Why was someone so anxious to get possession of it? Because it incriminated him. And what would he do with it? Thrust it into his pocket, most likely, never noticing that a corner of it had been left in the grip of the corpse. If we could get the rest of that sheet, we should have gone a long way towards solving the mystery."

"Yes, but how can we get at the criminal's pocket before we catch the criminal?"

"Well, well, it was worth thinking over. Then there is another obvious point. The note was sent to William. The man who wrote it could not have taken it to him, otherwise of course he might have delivered his own message by word of mouth. Who brought the note, then? Or did it come through the post?"

"I have made inquiries," said the inspector. "William received a letter by the afternoon post yesterday. The envelope was destroyed by him."

"Excellent!" cried Holmes, clapping him on the back. "It is a pleasure to work with you. Well, here is the lodge, and if you will come up, Colonel, I will show you the scene of the crime."

We passed the pretty cottage where the murdered man had lived, and walked up an oak-lined avenue to the fine old Queen Anne house. Holmes and the inspector led us round it to the side gate, which is separated by a stretch of garden from the hedge which lines the road. A constable was standing at the kitchen door.

"Throw the door open, officer," said Holmes. "Now it was on those stairs that young Mr. Cunningham stood and saw the two men struggling just where we are. Old Mr. Cunningham was at that window—the second on the left—and he saw the fellow get away just to the left of that bush. So did the son. They are both sure of it on account of the bush. Then Mister Alec ran out and knelt beside the wounded man. The ground is very hard, you see, and there are no marks to guide us."

As he spoke two men came down the garden path, from round the angle of the house. The one was elderly, with a strong, deep-lined, heavy-eyed face; the other a dashing young fellow, whose bright, smiling expression and showy dress were in strange contrast with the business which had brought us there.

"Still at it, then?" said the young man to Holmes. "I thought you Londoners were never at fault. You don't seem to be so quick after all."

"Ah! You must give us time," said Holmes good-humoredly.

"You'll want it," said young Alec Cunningham. "Why, I don't see that we have any clue at all."

"There's only one," answered the inspector. "We thought that if we could only find— Good heavens! Mr. Holmes, what is the matter?"

My poor friend's face had assumed the most dreadful expression. His eyes rolled upwards, his features writhed in agony, and with a suppressed groan he dropped upon the ground. Horrified, we carried him into the kitchen, where he lay back in a large chair and breathed heavily for some minutes. Finally, with a shame-faced apology for his weakness, he rose once more.

"Watson would tell you that I have just recovered from a severe illness," he explained. "I am liable to these sudden attacks."

"Shall I send you home in my trap?" asked old Cunningham.

"Well, since I am here there is one point which I should like verified. It seems to me that it is just possible that the arrival of this poor fellow William was not before but after the entrance of the burglar into the house. You appear to take it for granted that although the door was forced the robber never got in."

"I fancy that is quite obvious," said Mr. Cunningham gravely. "Why, my son Alec had not yet gone to bed, and he would certainly have heard anyone moving about."

"Where was he sitting?"

"I was sitting smoking in my dressing room."

"Which window is that?"

"The last on the left, next my father's."

"Both your lamps were lit, of course?"

"Undoubtedly."

"Is it not extraordinary," said Holmes, smiling, "that a burglar—and a burglar who had had some previous experience—should deliberately break into a house at a time when he could see from the lights that two of the family were still afoot?"

"If the case were not an odd one we should not have been driven to ask you for an explanation," said Mister Alec. "But as to your idea that the man had robbed the house before William tackled him, I think it most absurd. Shouldn't we have found the place disarranged and missed the things which he had taken?"

"It depends on what the things were," said Holmes. "You must remember that we are dealing with a burglar who is a very peculiar fellow, and who appears to work on lines of his own. Look, for example, at the queer lot of things which he took from Acton's."

"Well, we are quite in your hands, Mr. Holmes," said Mr. Cunningham. "Anything which you may suggest will certainly be done."

"In the first place," said Holmes, "I should like you to offer a reward—coming from yourself, for the officials may take a little time before they would agree upon the sum, and these things cannot be done too promptly. I have jotted down the form here, if you would not mind signing it. Fifty pounds is quite enough."

"I would willingly give five hundred," said the squire, taking the slip of paper and the pencil which Holmes handed to him. "This is not quite correct, however," he added, glancing over the document. You begin: 'Whereas, at about a quarter to one on Tuesday morning, an attempt was made'—and so on. It was at a quarter to twelve, as a matter of fact."

I was pained at the mistake, for I knew how keenly Holmes would feel any slip of the kind. It was his specialty to be accurate as to fact, but his recent illness had shaken him, and this one little incident was enough to show me that he was still far from being himself. He was obviously embarrassed for an instant, while the inspector raised his eyebrows and Alec Cunningham burst into a laugh. The old gentleman corrected the mistake, however, and handed the paper back to Holmes.

"Get it printed as soon as possible," he said. "I think your idea is an excellent one."

Holmes put the slip of paper carefully away in his pocketbook. "And now," said he, "it would really be a good thing that we should all go over the house together, and make certain that this erratic burglar did not, after all, carry anything away."

Before examining the rest of the house, Holmes studied the door which had been forced. It was evident that a chisel or strong knife had been thrust in, and the lock forced back with it. We could see the marks in the wood where it had been pushed in.

"You don't keep a dog?" he asked.

"Yes; but he is chained on the other side of the house."

"When do the servants go to bed?"

"About ten."

"Now, I should be very glad if you would have the kindness to show us over the house, Mr. Cunningham."

A stone-flagged passage, with the kitchens branching away from it, led by a wooden staircase directly to the second floor of the house. It came out upon the landing opposite to another more ornamental stair which led up from the front hall. Out of this landing opened the drawing room and several bedrooms, including those of Mr. Cunningham and his son. Holmes walked slowly, taking keen note of the architecture of the house. I could tell from his expression that he was on a hot scent, and yet I could not in the least imagine in what direction his inferences were leading him.

"My good sir," said Mr. Cunningham with some impatience, "this is surely very unnecessary. That is my room at the end of the stairs, and my son's is the one beyond it. I leave it to your judgment whether it was possible for the thief to have come up here without disturbing us."

"You must try round and get on a fresh scent, I fancy," said the son with a rather malicious smile.

"Still, I must ask you to humor me a little further. I should like, for example, to see how far the windows of the bedrooms command the front. This, I understand, is your son's room"—he pushed open the door—"and that, I presume, is the dressing room in which he sat smoking when the alarm was given. Where does the window of that look out to?" He stepped across the bedroom, pushed open the door, and glanced round the other chamber.

"I hope you are satisfied now?" said Mr. Cunningham testily.

"Thank you; I think I have seen all that I wished."

"Then, if it is really necessary, we can go into my room."

"If it is not too much trouble."

The squire shrugged his shoulders, and led the way into his chamber, which was a plainly furnished and commonplace room. As we moved across it in the direction of the window, Holmes fell back until he and I were the last of the group. Near the foot of the bed was a small square table, on which stood a dish of oranges and a carafe of water. As we passed it, Holmes, to my unutterable astonishment, leaned over in front of me and deliberately knocked the whole thing over. The glass smashed into a thousand pieces, and the fruit rolled into every corner of the room. "You've done it now, Watson," said he, coolly. "A pretty mess you've made."

I stooped in some confusion and began to pick up the fruit, understanding that for some reason my companion desired me to take the blame upon myself. The others set the table on its legs again.

"Halloa!" cried the inspector. "Where's he got to?"

Holmes had disappeared.

"Wait here an instant," said young Alec Cunningham. "The fellow is off his head, in my opinion. Come with me, Father, and see where he has got to!" They rushed out of the room, leaving the inspector, the colonel, and me, staring at each other.

"'Pon my word, I am inclined to agree with Mister Alec," said the official. "It may be the effect of this illness, but it seems to me that—"

His words were cut short by a scream of "Help! Help! Murder!" I recognized the voice as that of my friend, and I rushed madly from the room onto the landing, with the inspector and the colonel close behind. The cries, which had sunk down into a hoarse, inarticulate shouting, came from the room which we had first visited. I dashed in, and on into the dressing room beyond. The two Cunninghams were bending over the prostrate figure of Holmes, the younger clutching his throat with both hands, while the elder seemed to be twisting one of his wrists. In an instant the three of us had torn them away from him, and Holmes staggered to his feet, very pale, and evidently greatly exhausted.

"Arrest these men, Inspector!" he gasped.

"On what charge?"

"That of murdering their coachman, William Kirwan!"

"Oh, come now, Mr. Holmes," said the inspector. "I am sure you don't really mean to—"

"Tut, man, look at their faces!" cried Holmes curtly.

Never, certainly, have I seen a plainer confession of guilt upon human countenances. The older man seemed numbed and dazed, with a heavy, sullen expression upon his strongly marked face.

The son, on the other hand, had dropped all that jaunty, dashing style which had characterized him, and the ferocity of a dangerous wild beast gleamed in his dark eyes and distorted his handsome features. The inspector said nothing, but, stepping to the door, he blew his whistle. Two of his constables came at the call.

"I have no alternative, Mr. Cunningham," said he. "I trust that this may all prove to be an absurd mistake; but you can see that— Ah would you? Drop it!" He struck out with his hand, and a revolver, which the younger man was in the act of cocking, clattered down upon the floor.

"Keep that," said Holmes, quickly putting his foot upon it. "You will find it useful at the trial. But this is what we really wanted." He held up a little crumpled piece of paper.

"The remainder of the sheet?" cried the inspector.

"Precisely."

"And where was it?"

"Where I was sure it must be. I'll make the whole matter clear to you presently. I think, Colonel, that you and Watson might return now. The inspector and I must have a word with the prisoners; but you will certainly see me back at lunchtime."

HOLMES WAS AS GOOD as his word, for about one o'clock he rejoined us in the colonel's smoking room. He was accompanied by a little elderly gentleman, who was introduced to me as Mr. Acton whose house had been the scene of the original burglary.

"I wished Mr. Acton to be present while I demonstrated this small matter to you," said Holmes. "It is natural that he should take a keen interest in the details. I am afraid, my dear Colonel, that you must regret having taken in such a stormy petrel as I am."

"On the contrary," answered the colonel warmly, "I consider it the greatest privilege to have been permitted to study your methods of working. I confess that they quite surpass my expectations, and that I am utterly unable to account for your result."

"I am afraid that my explanation may disillusion you," said Holmes; "but it has always been my habit to hide none of my methods, either from my friend Watson or from anyone who might take an intelligent interest in them. Pray interrupt me if there is any inference which is not perfectly clear to you.

"It is of the highest importance in the art of detection to be able to recognize, out of a number of facts, which are incidental and which vital. Otherwise your energy and attention must be dissipated instead of being concentrated. Now, in this case there was not the slightest doubt in my mind from the first that the key of the whole matter lay in the scrap of paper in the dead man's hand. If Alec Cunningham's narrative were correct, and if the assailant after shooting William Kirwan had *instantly* fled, then it obviously could not be he who tore the paper from the dead man's hand. But if it was not he, it must have been Alex Cunningham himself, for by the time the old man had descended, several servants were upon the scene. The point is a simple one, but the inspector had overlooked it because he had started with the supposition that these county magnates had had nothing to do with the matter. Now, I make a point of never having any prejudices and of following docilely wherever fact may lead me, and so I found myself looking a little askance at the part which had been played by Mister Alec.

"And now I made a careful examination of the corner of paper which the inspector had submitted to us. It was at once clear to me that it formed part of a remarkable document. Here it is. Do you now observe something very suggestive about it?"

"It has a very irregular look," said the colonel.

"My dear sir," cried Holmes, "there cannot be the least doubt in the world that it has been written by two persons doing alternate words. When I draw your attention to the strong t's of 'at' and 'to' and ask you to compare them with the weak ones of 'quarter' and 'twelve,' you will instantly recognize the fact. A very brief analysis of those four words would enable you to say with the utmost confidence that the 'learn' and the 'maybe' are written in the stronger hand, and the 'what' in the weaker."

"By Jove, it's as clear as day!" cried the colonel. "Why on earth should two men write a letter in such a fashion?"

"Obviously the business was a bad one, and one of the men

who distrusted the other was determined that, whatever was done, each should have an equal hand in it. Now, of the two men, it is clear that the one who wrote the 'at' and 'to' was the ringleader."

"How do you get at that?"

"We might deduce it from the mere character of the one hand as compared with the other. But we have more assured reasons than that for supposing it. If you examine this scrap with attention you will come to the conclusion that the man with the stronger hand wrote all his words first, leaving blanks for the other to fill up. These blanks were not always sufficient, and the second man had a squeeze to fit his 'quarter' in between the 'at' and the 'to,' showing that the latter were already written. The man who wrote all his words first is undoubtedly the man who planned this affair."

"Excellent!" cried Mr. Acton.

"But very superficial," said Holmes. "We come now, however, to a point which is of importance. You may not be aware that the deduction of a man's age from his writing is one which has been brought to considerable accuracy by experts. In normal cases one can place a man in his true decade with tolerable confidence. I say normal cases, because ill health and physical weakness reproduce the signs of old age, even when the invalid is a youth. In this case, looking at the bold, strong hand of the one, and the rather broken-backed appearance of the other, we can say that the one was a young man, and the other was advanced in years."

"Excellent!" cried Mr. Acton again.

"There is a further point which is subtler and of greater interest. There is something in common between these hands. They belong to men who are blood relatives. It may be most obvious to you in the Greek e's, but there are many small points which indicate the same thing. They all tended to deepen my impression that the Cunninghams, father and son, had written this letter.

"I next went up to the house with the inspector, and saw all that was to be seen. The wound upon the dead man was, as I was able to determine with absolute confidence, caused by a shot from a revolver fired at a distance of something over four yards. There was no powder blackening on the clothes. Evidently, therefore,

Alec Cunningham had lied when he said that the two men were struggling when the shot was fired. Again, both father and son agreed as to the place where the man escaped into the road. At that point, however, there is a broad ditch, moist at the bottom. As there were no indications of bootmarks about this ditch, I was sure that the Cunninghams had again lied, and that there had never been any unknown man upon the scene.

"And now I had to consider the motive of this singular crime. I endeavored first of all to solve the reason for the original burglary at Mr. Acton's. I understood from something which the colonel told us that a lawsuit had been going on between you, Mr. Acton, and the Cunninghams. Of course, it instantly occurred to me that they had broken into your library with the intention of getting at some document which might be of importance in the case."

"Precisely so," said Mr. Acton. "There can be no possible doubt as to their intentions. I have the clearest claim upon half their present estate, and if they could have found a single paper—which, fortunately, was in the strongbox of my solicitors—they would undoubtedly have crippled our case."

"There you are!" said Holmes, smiling. "It was a dangerous, reckless attempt, in which I seemed to trace the influence of young Alec. Having found nothing, they tried to divert suspicion by making it appear to be an ordinary burglary, to which end they carried off whatever they could lay their hands upon. That is all clear enough, but there was much that was still obscure. What I wanted above all was to get the missing part of that note. I was certain that Alec had torn it out of the dead man's hand, and almost certain that he must have thrust it into the pocket of his dressing gown. Where else could he have put it? The only question was whether it was still there. It was worth an effort to find out, and for that object we all went up to the house.

"The Cunninghams joined us, as you doubtless remember, outside the kitchen door. It was, of course, of the very first importance that they should not be reminded of the existence of this paper, otherwise they would naturally destroy it without delay. The inspector was about to tell them the importance which was attached to it when, by the luckiest chance in the world, I tumbled down in a sort of fit and so changed the conversation."

"Good heavens!" cried the colonel, laughing. "Do you mean to say all our sympathy was wasted and your fit an imposture?"

"Speaking professionally, it was admirably done," cried I, looking in amazement at this man who was forever confounding me with some new phase of his astuteness.

"It is an art which is often useful," said he. "When I recovered I managed by a device, which had, perhaps, some little merit of ingenuity, to get old Cunningham to write the word 'twelve,' so that I might compare it with the 'twelve' upon the paper."

"Oh, what an ass I have been!" I exclaimed.

"I could see that you were commiserating with me over my weakness," said Holmes, laughing. "I was sorry to cause you the sympathetic pain which I know that you felt. We then went upstairs together, and having entered the room, and seen the dressing gown hanging up behind the door, I contrived by upsetting a table to engage their attention for the moment and slipped back to examine the pockets. I had hardly got the paper, however, which was, as I had expected, in one of them, when the two Cunninghams were on me, and would, I verily believe, have murdered me then and there but for your prompt and friendly aid. As it is, I feel that young man's grip on my throat now. They saw that I must know all about it, and the sudden change from absolute security to complete despair made them desperate.

"I had a little talk with old Cunningham afterwards as to the motive of the crime. He was tractable enough, though his son was a perfect demon, ready to blow out his own or anybody else's brains if he could have used his revolver. When Cunningham saw that the case against him was so strong he lost all heart, and made a clean breast of everything. It seems that William had secretly followed his two masters when they made their raid upon Mr. Acton's, and proceeded to blackmail them. Mister Alec, however, was a dangerous man to play games of that sort with. It was a stroke of positive genius on his part to see in the burglary scare, which was convulsing the countryside, an opportunity of getting rid of the man whom he feared. William was decoyed up and shot; and, had they only got the whole of the note, and paid a little more attention to detail in their accessories, it is possible that suspicion might never have been aroused."

"And the note?" I asked.

If you will only come round at quarter to twelve to the East gate you will learn what will very much surprise you and maybe be of the greatest service to you and also to Annie Morrison But say nothing to anyone upon the matter

Sherlock Holmes placed the subjoined paper before us. "It is very much the sort of thing that I expected," said he. "Of course, we do not yet know what the relations may have been between Alec Cunningham, William Kirwan, and this Annie Morrison. The result shows that the trap was skillfully baited. I am sure that you cannot fail to be delighted with the traces of heredity shown in the p's and in the tails of the g's. The absence of the i-dots in the old man's writing is also most characteristic. Watson, I think our quiet rest in the country has been a distinct success, and I shall return, much invigorated, to Baker Street tomorrow."

✔

In time Dr. Watson married and resumed the practice of medicine. He called often upon his friend, Sherlock Holmes, however, and continued to share in and to record his adventures.

I HAD CALLED UPON Sherlock Holmes on the second morning after Christmas, with the intention of wishing him the compliments of the season. He was lounging upon the sofa in a purple dressing gown, a pipe rack within his reach, and a pile of crumpled morning papers near at hand. Beside the couch was a wooden chair, and on the angle of the back hung a very seedy and disreputable hard felt hat. A lens and a forceps lying upon the seat of the chair suggested that the hat had been suspended in this manner for the purpose of examination.

"You are engaged," said I; "perhaps I interrupt you."

"Not at all. I am glad to have a friend with whom I can discuss my results. The matter is a trivial one"—he jerked his thumb in the direction of the old hat—"but there are points in connection with it which are not entirely devoid of interest."

I warmed my hands before his crackling fire, then seated myself in his armchair, which was drawn up to the window. "I suppose," I remarked, "that this homely thing is the clue which will guide you in the solution of some mystery, and the punishment of some crime."

"No, no. No crime," said Sherlock Holmes, laughing. "Only one of those whimsical little incidents which will happen when you have four million human beings all jostling each other within the space of a few square miles. You know Peterson, the commissionaire?"

"Yes."

"It is he who found this trophy. About four o'clock on Christmas morning, he was returning from some small jollification, and was making his way homewards down Tottenham Court Road. In front of him he saw, in the gaslight, a tallish man, walking with a slight stagger, and carrying a white goose slung over his shoulder. At the corner of Goodge Street a row broke out between this stranger and a little knot of roughs. One of the latter knocked off the man's hat, on which he raised his stick to defend himself, and, swinging it over his head, smashed the shopwindow behind him. Peterson rushed forward to protect the stranger from his assailants, but the man, shocked at having broken the window and seeing an official-looking person in uniform rushing towards him, dropped his goose, took to his heels, and vanished amid the labyrinth of small streets which lie at the back of Tottenham Court Road. The roughs also fled, so that Peterson was left in possession of this battered hat and a most unimpeachable Christmas goose."

"Which surely he restored to their owner?"

"My dear fellow, there lies the problem. It is true that FOR MRS. HENRY BAKER was printed upon a small card which was tied to the bird's left leg, and that the initials H.B. are legible upon the lining of this hat; but, as there are some thousands of Bakers, and some hundreds of Henry Bakers in our city, it is not easy to restore lost property to any one of them. So Peterson brought round both hat and goose to me on Christmas Day, knowing that even the smallest problems are of interest to me. The goose we retained until this morning, when there were signs that, in spite of the slight frost, it would be well that it should be eaten without delay. Its finder has carried it off, therefore, to fulfill the ultimate destiny of a goose, while I retain the hat of the unknown gentleman who lost his Christmas dinner."

"What clue could you have as to his identity?"

"Only as much as we can deduce from his hat. Here is my lens. You know my methods. What can you gather yourself as to the individuality of the man who wore this article?"

I took the tattered object in my hands, and turned it over rather ruefully. It was a very ordinary round black hat, much the worse for wear. The lining had been of red silk, but was a good deal discolored. There was no maker's name; but, as Holmes had remarked, the initials H.B. were scrawled upon one side.

For the rest, it was cracked, exceedingly dusty, and spotted in several places, although there seemed to have been some attempt to hide the discolored patches by smearing them with ink.

"I can see nothing," said I, handing it back to my friend.

"On the contrary, Watson, you can see everything. You fail, however, to draw inferences from what you see."

"Then, pray tell me what it is that you infer from this hat?"

He picked it up, and gazed at it in the peculiar introspective fashion which was characteristic of him. "That the man was highly intellectual is obvious upon the face of it, and also that he was fairly well-to-do within the last three years, although he has now fallen upon evil days, probably the work of drink upon him. This may account also for the fact that his wife has ceased to love him."

"My dear Holmes!"

"He has, however, retained some degree of self-respect," he continued, disregarding my remonstrance. "He is a man who leads a sedentary life, goes out little, is out of training entirely, is middle-aged, has grizzled hair which he has had cut within the last few days, and which he anoints with lime cream. Also, it is extremely improbable that he has gas laid on in his house."

"I must confess that I am unable to follow you. For example, how did you deduce that this man was intellectual?"

For answer Holmes clapped the hat upon his head. It came right over the forehead and settled upon the bridge of his nose. "It is a question of cubic capacity," said he. "A man with so large a brain must have something in it."

"The decline of his fortunes, then?"

"This hat is three years old. These flat brims curled at the edge came in then. It is a hat of the best quality. Look at the band of ribbed silk, and the excellent lining. If this man could afford to buy so expensive a hat three years ago, and has had no hat since, then he has assuredly gone down in the world. On the other hand, he has endeavored to conceal some of these stains upon the felt by daubing them with ink, which is a sign that he has not entirely lost his self-respect."

"Your reasoning is certainly plausible."

"The further points that he is middle-aged, that his hair is grizzled, that it has been recently cut, and that he uses lime cream, are all to be gathered from a close examination of the lower part of the lining. The lens discloses a large number of hair ends, clean-cut by the scissors of the barber. They appear to be adhesive, and there is a distinct odor of lime cream. This dust, you will observe, is not the gritty gray dust of the street, but the fluffy brown dust of the house, showing that it has been hung up indoors most of the time; while the marks of moisture upon the inside are proof that the wearer perspired freely, and could, therefore, hardly be in the best of training."

"But his wife—you said that she had ceased to love him."

"That hat has not been brushed for weeks. When I see you, Watson, with a week's accumulation of dust upon your hat, and when your wife allows you to go out in such a state, I shall fear that you also have been unfortunate enough to lose your wife's affection."

"But he might be a bachelor."

"Nay, he was bringing home the goose to his wife! Remember the card upon the bird's leg."

"But how do you deduce that gas is not laid on in the house?"

"One tallow stain, or even two, might come by chance; but, when I see no less than five, I think that there can be little doubt that the individual must be brought into frequent contact with burning tallow—walks upstairs at night probably with his hat in one hand and a guttering candle in the other. Anyhow, he never got tallow stains from a gas jet. Are you satisfied?"

"Well, it is very ingenious," said I, laughing; "but since, as you said, there has been no crime committed, and no harm done save the loss of a goose, all this seems rather a waste of energy."

Holmes had opened his mouth to reply, when the door flew open, and Peterson, the commissionaire, rushed into the room.

"The goose, Mr. Holmes! The goose, sir!" he gasped. "See what my wife found in its crop!" He held out his hand, and displayed in the center of the palm a brilliantly scintillating blue stone, rather smaller than a bean in size, but of such purity and radiance that it twinkled like an electric point in the dark hollow of his hand.

Holmes sat up with a whistle. "By Jove, Peterson, this is treasure trove indeed! I suppose you know what you have got?"

"A precious stone, sir! It cuts into glass as though it were putty."

"It's more than a precious stone. It's *the* precious stone."

"Not the Countess of Morcar's Blue Carbuncle?" I ejaculated.

"Precisely so. I ought to know its size and shape, seeing that I have read the advertisement about it in *The Times* every day lately. It is absolutely unique, and its value can only be conjectured, but the reward offered of a thousand pounds is certainly not within a twentieth part of the market price."

"A thousand pounds! Great Lord of mercy!" Peterson plumped down into a chair, and stared from one to the other of us.

"It was lost, if I remember aright, at the Hotel Cosmopolitan," I remarked.

"On the twenty-second of December, just five days ago. I have some account of the matter here, I believe." Holmes rummaged amid his newspapers, glancing over the dates, until at last he smoothed one out, doubled it over, and read:

"Hotel Cosmopolitan Jewel Robbery

John Horner, 26, plumber, was brought up upon the charge of having, upon the 22nd inst., abstracted from the jewel case of the Countess of Morcar the valuable gem known as the Blue Carbuncle. James Ryder, head attendant at the hotel, gave his evidence to the effect that he had shown Horner up to the dressing room of the Countess of Morcar upon the day of the robbery, in order that he might solder the second bar of the grate, which was loose. He had remained with Horner some little time but had finally been called away.

On returning he found that Horner had disappeared, that the bureau had been forced open, and that the small morocco casket in which, as it afterwards transpired, the Countess was accustomed to keep her jewel, was lying empty upon the dressing table. Ryder instantly gave the alarm, and Horner was arrested the same evening; but the stone could not be found either upon his person or in his rooms. Catherine Cusack, maid to the Countess, deposed to having heard Ryder's cry of dismay on discovering the robbery, and to having rushed into the room, where she found matters were as described by the last witness. Inspector Bradstreet, B Division, gave evidence as to the arrest of Horner, who struggled frantically and protested his innocence in the strongest terms. Evidence of a previous conviction for robbery having been given against the prisoner, the magistrate refused to deal summarily with the offense, but referred it to the assizes.

"Hum! So much for the police court," said Holmes thoughtfully, tossing aside his paper. "The question for us now to solve is the sequence of events leading from a rifled jewel case at one end to the crop of a goose in Tottenham Court Road at the other. You see, Watson, our little deductions have suddenly assumed a much less innocent aspect. Here is the stone; the stone came from the goose, and the goose came from Mr. Henry Baker, the gentleman with the bad hat and all the characteristics with which I have bored you. So now we must set ourselves to finding this gentleman, and ascertaining what part he has played in this little mystery. To do this, we must try the simplest means first, and these lie undoubtedly in an advertisement in all the evening papers."

"What will you say?"

"Give me a pencil, and that slip of paper. Now, then: 'Found at the corner of Goodge Street, a goose and a black felt hat. Mr. Henry Baker can have the same by applying at six thirty this evening at 221 B Baker Street.' That is clear and concise."

"Very. But will he see it?"

"Well, he is sure to keep an eye on the papers, since, to a poor man, the loss was a heavy one. He was clearly so scared by his mischance in breaking the window, and by the approach of Peterson, that he thought of nothing but flight; but since then he must have bitterly regretted the impulse which caused him to drop his bird. Then again, the introduction of his name will cause everyone who knows him to direct his attention to it. Here you are, Peterson, run out and have this put in the evening papers."

"Very well, sir. And this stone?"

"Ah, yes, I shall keep the stone. Thank you. And, I say, Peterson, just buy a goose on your way back and leave it here with me, for we must have one to give to this gentleman in place of the one which your family is now devouring."

When the commissionaire had gone, Holmes held the stone against the light. "It's a bonny thing," said he. "Just see how it glints and sparkles. Of course it is a nucleus and focus of crime. Every good stone is. They are the devil's pet baits. In the larger and older jewels every facet may stand for a bloody deed. This stone is not yet twenty years old. It was found in the banks of the Amoy River in southern China, and is remarkable in having every characteristic of the carbuncle, save that it is blue, instead of ruby red. In spite of its youth, it has already a sinister history. There have been two murders, a vitriol throwing, a suicide, and several robberies for the sake of this forty-grain weight of crystallized carbon. Who would think that so pretty a toy would be a purveyor to the gallows and the prison? I'll lock it up in my strongbox, and drop the Countess a line to say that we have it."

"Do you think this man Horner is innocent?"

"I cannot tell."

"Well, then, do you imagine that this other one, Henry Baker, had anything to do with the matter?"

"It is, I think, much more likely that Henry Baker is an absolutely innocent man, who had no idea that the bird which he was carrying was of considerably more value than if it were made of solid gold. That I shall determine by a very simple test, but not until we have an answer to our advertisement."

"In that case I shall continue my professional round. But I shall come back in the evening, for I should like to see the solution of so tangled a business."

"Very glad to see you. I dine at seven. There is a woodcock, I believe. By the way, in view of recent occurrences, perhaps I ought to ask Mrs. Hudson to examine its crop."

I HAD BEEN DELAYED at a case, and it was after half past six when I found myself in Baker Street once more. As I approached the house I saw a man waiting outside in the bright semicircle of light which was thrown from the fanlight. Just as I arrived, the door was opened, and we were shown up together to Holmes's room.

"Mr. Henry Baker, I believe," said he, rising from his armchair, and greeting his visitor with the easy air of geniality which he could so readily assume. "Pray take this chair by the fire, Mr. Baker. Ah, Watson, you have just come at the right time. Is that your hat, Mr. Baker?"

"Yes, sir, that is undoubtedly my hat." He was a large man, with rounded shoulders, a massive head, and a broad, intelligent face, sloping down to a pointed beard of grizzled brown. A touch

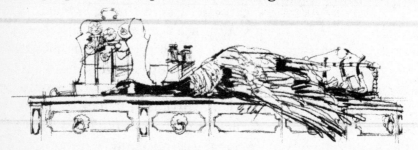

of red in nose and cheeks, with a slight tremor of his extended hand, recalled Holmes's surmise as to his habits. His rusty black frock coat was buttoned right up in front, with the collar turned up, and his lank wrists protruded from his sleeves without a sign of cuff or shirt. He spoke in a low staccato fashion, choosing his words with care, and gave the impression of a man of learning who had had ill-usage at the hands of fortune.

"We have retained these things for some days," said Holmes, "because we expected to see an advertisement from you giving your address. I am at a loss to know why you did not advertise."

Our visitor gave a rather shamefaced laugh. "Shillings have not been so plentiful with me as they once were," he remarked. "I had no doubt that the gang of roughs who assaulted me had carried off both my hat and the bird. I did not care to spend more money in a hopeless attempt at recovering them."

"Naturally. By the way, we were compelled to eat the bird."

"To eat it!" Our visitor half rose from his chair.

"Yes; it would have been no use to anyone had we not done so. But I presume that this goose upon the sideboard, which is about the same weight and perfectly fresh, will answer your purpose equally well?"

"Oh, certainly!" answered Mr. Baker, with a sigh of relief.

"Of course, we still have the feathers, legs, crop, and so on of your own bird, if you so wish—"

The man burst into a hearty laugh. "I think, sir, that with your permission I will confine my attentions to the excellent bird which I perceive upon the sideboard."

Sherlock Holmes glanced sharply across at me with a slight shrug of his shoulders. "There is your hat, then, and there your bird," said he. "By the way, would you tell me where you got the other one from? I have seldom seen a better-grown goose."

"Certainly, sir," said Baker, who had risen and tucked his newly gained property under his arm. "There are a few of us who frequent the Alpha Inn near the Museum—we are to be found in the Museum itself during the day, you understand. This year our good host instituted a goose club, by which, on consideration of some few pence every week, we were to receive a bird at Christmas. My pence were paid, and the rest is familiar to you. I am much indebted to you, sir." With a comical pomposity of manner he bowed solemnly to both of us, and strode off upon his way.

"So much for Mr. Henry Baker," said Holmes, when he had closed the door behind him. "It is quite certain that he knows nothing whatever about the matter. Are you hungry, Watson?"

"Not particularly."

"Then I suggest that we turn our dinner into a supper, and follow up this clue while it is still hot."

It was a bitter night, so we drew on our ulsters and wrapped cravats about our throats. Outside, the stars were shining coldly in a cloudless sky, and the breath of the passersby blew out into smoke like so many pistol shots. Our footfalls rang out crisply and loudly as we swung through the doctors' quarter, Wimpole Street, Harley Street, and so through Wigmore Street into Oxford Street. In a quarter of an hour we were in Bloomsbury at the Alpha Inn, which is a small public house at the corner of one of the streets which runs down into Holborn. Holmes pushed open the door of the bar, and ordered two glasses of beer from the ruddy-faced, white-aproned landlord.

"Your beer should be excellent if it is as good as your geese," he said.

"My geese!" The man seemed surprised.

"Yes. I was speaking only half an hour ago to Mr. Henry Baker, who was a member of your goose club."

"Ah! Yes, I see. But you see, sir, them's not *our* geese."

"Indeed! Whose, then?"

"I get them from Breckinridge in Covent Garden."

"Ah! Well, here's your good health, landlord, and prosperity to your house. Good night.

"Now for Mr. Breckinridge," he continued, buttoning up his coat, as we came out into the frosty air. "Remember, Watson, that though we have so homely a thing as a goose at one end of this chain, we have at the other a man who will certainly get seven years' penal servitude, unless we can establish his innocence. Faces to the south, and quick march!"

We passed across Holborn and through a zigzag of slums to Covent Garden Market. One of the largest stalls bore the name of Breckinridge upon it, and the proprietor, a man with a sharp face and trim side-whiskers, was putting up the shutters.

"Good evening. Sold out of geese, I see," said Holmes, pointing at the bare slabs of marble.

"There are some on the stall with the gas flare," said the salesman.

"But I was recommended to you by the landlord of the Alpha."

"Ah, yes. I sent him a couple of dozen."

"Fine birds they were, too. Now where did you get them from?"

To my surprise the question provoked a burst of anger from the salesman. "Now then, mister," said he, with his head cocked and his arms akimbo, "what are you driving at? I shan't tell you. So now!"

"Oh, it is a matter of no importance; but I don't know why you should be so warm over such a trifle."

"Warm! You'd be as warm, maybe, if you were as pestered as

I am. It's 'Where are the geese?' and 'Who did you sell the geese to?' and 'What will you take for the geese?' One would think they were the only geese in the world."

"Well, if you won't tell us the bet is off," said Holmes carelessly. "But I'm always ready to back my opinion on a matter of fowls, and I have a fiver on it that the bird I ate is country-bred."

"Well, then, you've lost your fiver," snapped the salesman. "All those birds that went to the Alpha were town-bred."

"You'll never persuade me to believe that."

"Will you bet, then?"

"It's merely taking your money. But I'll have a sovereign on with you, just to teach you not to be obstinate."

The salesman chuckled grimly. "Bring me the books, Bill," said he. A small boy brought round a thin volume and a great greasy-backed one, laying them beneath the hanging lamp.

"Now then, Mr. Cocksure," said the salesman, "you see this little book? That's the list of the folk from whom I buy. Here on this page are the countryfolk, and the numbers after their names are where their accounts are in the big ledger. Now, then! You see this other page in red ink? Well, that is a list of my town suppliers. Now read that third name out to me."

"Mrs. Oakshott, 117 Brixton Road—249," read Holmes.

"Quite so. Now turn that up in the ledger."

Holmes turned to the page indicated. "Here you are, 'Mrs. Oakshott, 117 Brixton Road, egg and poultry supplier.'"

"Now, then, what's the last entry?"

"'December twenty-two. Twenty-four geese at seven shillings sixpence. Sold to Mr. Windigate of the Alpha at twelve shillings.'"

"What have you to say now?"

Sherlock Holmes looked deeply chagrined. He drew a sovereign from his pocket and threw it down upon the slab, turning away with the air of a man whose disgust is too deep for words. A few yards off he stopped under a lamppost, and laughed in the hearty, noiseless fashion which was peculiar to him.

"When you see a man with whiskers of that cut, you can always draw him by a bet," said he. "I daresay that if I had put a hundred pounds down in front of him that man would not have given me such complete information as was drawn from him by the idea that he was doing me on a wager. Well, Watson, it is clear from what that surly fellow said that there are others besides ourselves who are anxious about the matter, and I should—"

His remarks were cut short by a loud hubbub which broke out from the stall he had just left. Turning round we saw a little rat-faced fellow standing in the circle of light which was thrown by the swinging lamp, while Breckinridge, framed in the door of his stall, was shaking his fists at the cringing figure.

"I've had enough of you and your geese," he shouted. "You bring Mrs. Oakshott here and I'll answer her, but what have you to do with it? Did I buy the geese off you?"

"No; but one of them was mine," whined the little man.

"Well, then, ask Mrs. Oakshott for it."

"She told me to ask you."

"Well, you can ask the King of Proosia, for all I care. I've had enough of it. Get out of this!" Breckinridge rushed fiercely forward, and the inquirer flitted away into the darkness.

"Ha, this may save us a visit to Brixton Road," whispered Holmes. "Come with me, and we will see what is to be made of this fellow." Striding through the scattered knots of people who lounged round the flaring stalls, my companion speedily overtook the little man and touched him upon the shoulder. He sprang round, and I could see in the gaslight that every vestige of color had been driven from his face.

"Who are you? What do you want?" he asked in a quavering voice.

"You will excuse me," said Holmes blandly, "but I could not help overhearing the questions which you put to the salesman just now. I think that I could be of assistance to you."

"You? Who are you? How could you know anything of the matter?"

"My name is Sherlock Holmes. It is my business to know what other people don't know. I believe that you are endeavoring to trace some geese which were sold by Mrs. Oakshott, of Brixton

Road, to a salesman named Breckinridge, by him to the landlord of the Alpha, and by him to his club of which Mr. Henry Baker is a member."

"Oh, sir, you are the very man whom I have longed to meet," cried the little fellow, with outstretched hands and quivering fingers. "I can hardly explain how interested I am in this matter."

Sherlock Holmes hailed a passing four-wheeler. "In that case we had better discuss it in a cozy room rather than in this wind-swept marketplace," said he. "But pray tell me, before we go further, who it is that I have the pleasure of assisting."

The man hesitated for an instant. "John Robinson," he answered, with a sidelong glance.

"No, no; the real name," said Holmes sweetly. "It is always awkward doing business with an alias."

A flush sprang to the white cheeks of the stranger. "Well, then," said he, "my real name is James Ryder."

"Precisely so. Head attendant at the Hotel Cosmopolitan. Pray step into the cab, and I shall soon be able to tell you everything which you would wish to know."

The little man stood glancing from one to the other of us with half-frightened, half-hopeful eyes, as one who is not sure whether he is on the verge of a windfall or of a catastrophe. Then he stepped into the cab, and in half an hour we were back at Baker Street. Nothing had been said during our drive, but the high, thin breathings of our new companion, and the claspings and unclaspings of his hands, spoke of his nervous tension.

"Here we are!" said Holmes cheerily, as we filed into the sitting room. "The fire looks very seasonable in this weather. You look cold, Mr. Ryder. Pray take the basket chair. I will just put on my slippers before we settle this little matter of yours. Now, then! You want to know what became of those geese? Or rather, I fancy, of one goose—white, with a black bar across the tail?"

Ryder quivered with emotion. "Oh, sir," he cried, "can you tell me where it went to?"

"It came here, and a most remarkable bird it proved. I don't wonder that you should take an interest in it. It laid an egg after it was dead—the bonniest, brightest little blue egg that ever was seen. I have it here in my museum."

Our visitor staggered to his feet, and clutched the mantelpiece with his right hand. Holmes unlocked his strongbox, and held up the Blue Carbuncle, which shone out like a star, with a cold, brilliant, many-pointed radiance. Ryder stood glaring with a drawn face, uncertain whether to claim or to disown it.

"The game's up, Ryder," said Holmes quietly. "Hold up, man, or you'll be into the fire. Help him back into his chair, Watson. He's not got blood enough to go in for felony with impunity."

For a moment Ryder had staggered and nearly fallen, but now he sat staring with frightened eyes at his accuser.

"I have almost every link in my hands, and all the proofs I need, so there is little which you need tell me. Still, that little may as well be cleared up to make the case complete. You had heard, Ryder, of this blue stone of the Countess of Morcar's?"

"Catherine Cusack told me of it," said he in a cracked voice.

"I see. Her ladyship's waiting maid. Well, the temptation of sudden wealth so easily acquired was too much for you, as it has been for better men before you; but you were not very scrupulous in the means you used. It seems to me, Ryder, that there is the makings of a very pretty villain in you. You knew that this man Horner, the plumber, had been concerned in some such matter before, and that suspicion would rest the more readily upon him. So you made some small job in my lady's room—you and your confederate Cusack—and you managed that he should be the man sent for. Then, when he had left, you rifled the jewel case, raised the alarm, and had this unfortunate man arrested. You then—"

Ryder threw himself down suddenly upon the rug, and clutched at my companion's knees. "For God's sake, have mercy!" he shrieked. "Think of my father! Of my mother! It would break their hearts. I never went wrong before! I never will again. I'll swear it on a Bible. Oh, don't bring it into court!"

"Get back into your chair!" said Holmes sternly. "It is very well to cringe and crawl now, but you thought little enough of poor Horner in the dock for a crime of which he knew nothing."

"I will fly, Mr. Holmes. I will leave the country, sir. Then the charge against him will break down."

"Hum! We will talk about that. Now, how came the stone into the goose, and how came the goose into the open market? Tell us the truth, for there lies your only hope of safety."

Ryder passed his tongue over his parched lips. "I will tell you it just as it happened, sir," said he. "When Horner had been arrested, it seemed to me that it would be best for me to get away with the stone at once, for I did not know at what moment the police might not take it into their heads to search me and my room, so I set out for my sister's house. She had married a man named Oakshott, and lived in Brixton Road, where she fattened fowls for the market. All the way there every man I met seemed to me to be a policeman, and for all that it was a cold night, the sweat was pouring down my face before I came to Brixton Road. My sister asked me what was the matter, and why I was so pale; but I told her that I had been upset by the robbery at the hotel. Then I went into the backyard, and smoked a pipe, and wondered what it would be best to do.

"I had a friend called Maudsley, who went to the bad, and has just been serving his time in Pentonville. He had often talked about the ways in which thieves could get rid of what they stole, so I made up my mind to go to Kilburn, where he lived, and take him into my confidence. He would show me how to turn the stone into money.

"But how to get to him in safety? I might at any moment be seized and searched, and there would be the stone in my pocket. I was leaning against the wall at the time, looking at the geese which were waddling about round my feet, and suddenly an idea came into my head.

"My sister had told me some weeks before that I might have the pick of her geese for a Christmas present. I would take my goose now, and in it I would carry my stone to Kilburn. There was a little shed in the yard, and behind this I drove one of the birds, a fine big one, white, with a barred tail. I caught it and, prizing its bill open, I thrust the stone down its throat as far as

123

my finger could reach. The bird gave a gulp, and I felt the stone pass along its gullet and down into its crop. But the creature flapped and struggled, and out came my sister to know what was the matter. As I turned to speak to her the brute broke loose, and fluttered off among the others.

"'Whatever were you doing with that bird, Jem?' says she.

"'Well,' said I, 'you said you'd give me one for Christmas, and I was feeling which was the fattest.'

"'Oh, very well, kill it and take it with you.'

"Well, I did what she said, and I carried the bird all the way to Kilburn. I told my pal what I had done, and he laughed until he choked. Then we got a knife and opened the goose. My heart turned to water, for there was no sign of the stone, and I knew that some terrible mistake had occurred. I rushed back to my sister's, and hurried into the backyard. There was not a bird to be seen.

"'Where are they all, Maggie?' I cried.

"'Gone to the dealer's.'

"'Which dealer's?'

"'Breckinridge, of Covent Garden.'

"'But was there another with a barred tail,' I asked, 'the same as the one I chose?'

"'Yes, Jem, there were two barred-tailed ones.'

"Well, then, of course, I saw it all, and I ran off as hard as my feet would carry me to this man Breckinridge; but he had sold the lot at once, and not one word would he tell me as to where they had gone. You heard him yourselves tonight. Well, he has always answered me like that. My sister thinks that I am going mad. Sometimes I think that I am myself. And now—and now I am myself a branded thief, without ever having touched the wealth for which I sold my character. God help me!" He burst into convulsive sobbing, with his face buried in his hands.

There was a long silence, broken only by his heavy breathing, and by the measured tapping of Holmes's fingertips upon the edge of the table. Then my friend rose, and threw open the door.

"Get out!" said he.

"What, sir! Oh, Heaven bless you!"

"No more words. Get out!"

And no more words were needed. There was a rush, a clatter upon the stairs, the bang of a door, and the crisp rattle of running footfalls from the street.

"After all, Watson," said Holmes, reaching up his hand for his clay pipe, "I am not retained by the police to supply their deficiencies. If Horner were in danger it would be another thing, but this fellow will not appear against him, and the case must collapse. I suppose that I am commuting a felony, but it is just possible that I am saving a soul. This fellow will not go wrong again. He is too terribly frightened. Send him to gaol now, and you make him a gaolbird for life. Besides, it is the season of forgiveness. Chance has put in our way a most singular and whimsical problem, and its solution is its own reward. If you will have the goodness to touch the bell, Doctor, we will begin another investigation, in which also a bird will be the chief feature."

Isa Whitney, brother of the late Elias Whitney, D.D., principal of the Theological College of St. George's, was much addicted to opium. The habit grew upon him, as I understand, from some foolish prank when he was at college, for having read De Quincey's description of his dreams and sensations, he had drenched his tobacco with laudanum in an attempt to produce the same effects. He found, as so many more have done, that the practice is easier to attain than to get rid of, and for many years he continued to be a slave to the drug, an object of mingled horror and pity to his friends and relatives. I can see him now, with yellow, pasty face, drooping lids and pinpoint pupils, all huddled in a chair, the wreck and ruin of a noble man.

One night—it was in June 1889—there came a ring to my bell, about the hour when a man gives his first yawn, and glances at the clock. I sat up in my chair, and my wife laid her needlework down in her lap and made a little face of disappointment.

"A patient!" she said. "You'll have to go out."

I groaned, for I was newly come back from a weary day.

We heard the door open, a few hurried words, and then quick steps upon the linoleum. Our own door flew open, and a lady, clad in some dark-colored stuff with a black veil, entered the room.

"You will excuse my calling so late," she began, and then, suddenly losing her self-control, she ran forward, threw her arms about my wife's neck, and sobbed upon her shoulder. "Oh! I'm in such trouble!" she cried. "I do so want a little help."

"Why," said my wife, pulling up her veil, "it is Kate Whitney. How you startled me, Kate! I did not know who you were when you came in."

"I didn't know what to do, so I came straight to you." That

was always the way. Folk who were in grief came to my wife like birds to a lighthouse.

"It was sweet of you to come. Now, you must tell us all about it. Or should you rather that I sent John off to bed?"

"Oh, no, no. I want the doctor's advice and help too. It's about Isa. He has not been home for two days. I am so frightened!"

It was not the first time that she had spoken to us of her husband's trouble, to me as a doctor, to my wife as an old friend and school companion. We soothed and comforted her by such words as we could find. Did she know where her husband was? Was it possible that we could bring him back to her?

It seemed that it was. She had the surest information that of late he had, when the fit was on him, made use of an opium den in the furthest east of the City. He was to be found, she was sure, at the Bar of Gold, in Upper Swandam Lane. But what was she to do? How could she, a young and timid woman, make her way into such a place, and pluck her husband out from among the ruffians who surrounded him?

There was the case, and of course there was but one way out of it. I was Isa Whitney's medical adviser, and as such I had influence over him. I would go to the address which she had given me and would send him home in a cab if he were indeed there. So in ten minutes I had left my armchair and my cheery sitting room, and was speeding eastward in a hansom on a strange errand, though the future only could show how strange it was to be.

Upper Swandam Lane is a vile alley lurking behind the high wharves which line the north side of the river to the east of London Bridge. Between a slop shop and a gin shop, approached by a steep flight of steps leading down to a black gap like the mouth of a cave, I found the den of which I was in search.

Ordering my cab to wait, I passed down the steps, and by the light of a flickering oil lamp above the door I found the latch and made my way into a long, low room, thick with brown opium smoke, and terraced with wooden berths, like the forecastle of an emigrant ship.

Through the gloom one could dimly catch a glimpse of bodies

lying in fantastic poses, bowed shoulders, bent knees, heads thrown back, with here and there a lackluster eye turned upon the newcomer. Out of the shadows there glimmered little red circles of light, now bright, now faint, as the burning poison waxed or waned in the bowls of the metal pipes. The most lay silent, but some talked together in low, monotonous voices, each mumbling out his own thoughts, and paying little heed to the words of his neighbor. At the further end was a small brazier of burning charcoal, beside which on a three-legged wooden stool there sat a tall, thin old man, with his jaw resting upon his two fists, and his elbows upon his knees, staring into the fire.

As I entered, a Malay attendant hurried up with a pipe for me and a supply of the drug, beckoning me to an empty berth.

"Thank you, I have not come to stay," said I. "There is a friend of mine here, Mr. Isa Whitney. I wish to speak with him."

There was a movement and an exclamation from my right, and, peering through the gloom, I saw Whitney, pale, haggard, and unkempt, staring out at me.

"My God! It's Watson," said he. He was in a pitiable state of reaction, with every nerve in a twitter. "I say, Watson, what o'clock is it? And what day?"

"Nearly eleven, Friday, June nineteenth."

"Good heavens! I thought it was Wednesday." He sank his face onto his arms, and began to sob in a high treble key.

"Your wife has been waiting these two days for you, man. You should be ashamed of yourself!"

"So I am. But you've got mixed, for I have only been here a few hours, three pipes, four pipes—I forget how many. But I'll go home with you. I wouldn't frighten Kate—poor little Kate. Find what I owe, Watson. I can do nothing for myself."

I walked down the narrow passage between the double row of sleepers, holding my breath to keep out the stupefying fumes of the drug, and looking about for the manager. As I passed the man who sat by the brazier I felt a pluck at my coat, and a low voice whispered, "Walk past me, and then look back." I glanced down. The words could only have come from the old man at my side, and yet he sat now as absorbed as ever, bent with age, an opium pipe dangling down from between his knees, as though it had dropped in sheer lassitude from his fingers.

I took two steps forward and looked back. It took all my self-control to prevent me from breaking into a cry of astonishment. He had turned his back so that none could see him but I. His form had filled out, his wrinkles were gone, the dull eyes had regained their fire, and there, sitting by the fire, and grinning at my surprise, was Sherlock Holmes.

"Holmes!" I whispered. "What on earth are you doing here?"

"As low as you can," he answered. "I have excellent ears. If you would have the kindness to get rid of that sottish friend of yours, I should be glad to have a little talk with you."

"I have a cab outside."

"Then pray send him home in it. I should recommend that you also send a note by the cabman to your wife to say that you have thrown in your lot with me. If you will wait outside, I shall be with you in five minutes."

It was difficult to refuse any of Sherlock Holmes's requests, and in a few minutes I had written my note, paid Whitney's bill, led him out to the cab, and seen him driven through the darkness. In a very short time a decrepit figure had emerged from the opium den, and I was walking down the street with Sherlock Holmes. For two streets he shuffled along with a bent back and an uncertain foot. Then, glancing quickly round, he straightened himself out and burst into a hearty fit of laughter.

"I suppose, Watson," said he, "that you imagine that I have added opium smoking to all my other little weaknesses."

"I was certainly surprised to find you there."

"But not more so than I to find you."

"I came to find a friend."

"And I to find an enemy! Briefly, Watson, I am in the midst of a very remarkable inquiry, and I hoped to find a clue in the incoherent ramblings of these sots, as I have done before now. Had I been recognized in that den my life would not have been worth an hour's purchase, for I have used it before now for my own purposes, and the rascally lascar who runs it has sworn vengeance upon me. There is a trapdoor at the back of that building, near the corner of Paul's Wharf, which could tell some strange tales of what has passed through it upon moonless nights."

"What! You do not mean bodies?"

"Aye, bodies, Watson. But our carriage should be here!" He put his two forefingers between his teeth and whistled shrilly, a signal which was answered by a similar whistle from the distance, followed by the rattle of wheels and the clink of a horse's hoofs.

"Now, Watson," said Holmes, as a tall dogcart dashed up through the gloom, throwing out two golden tunnels of yellow light from its side lanterns, "you'll come with me, won't you?"

"But I am all in the dark."

"You'll know all about it presently. Jump up here! All right, John, we shall not need you. Here's half-a-crown. Look out for me tomorrow about eleven."

He flicked the horse with his whip, and we dashed away through the endless succession of somber and deserted streets, which widened gradually, until we were flying across a broad balustraded bridge, with the murky river flowing sluggishly beneath us. Beyond lay another wilderness of bricks and mortar. A dull rack was drifting slowly across the sky, and a star or two twinkled dimly here and there through the rifts of the clouds. Holmes drove in silence, lost in thought, whilst I sat beside him curious to learn what this new quest might be, and yet afraid to break in upon the current of his thoughts. We had driven several miles and were beginning to get to the fringe of the belt of suburban villas, when he shook himself, shrugged, and lit up his pipe with the air of a man who has satisfied himself that he is acting for the best.

"You have a grand gift of silence, Watson," said he. "It makes you quite invaluable as a companion. 'Pon my word, it is a great thing for me to have someone to talk to, for my own thoughts are not overpleasant. I was wondering what I should say to this dear little woman when she sees me again at the door."

"You forget that I know nothing about it."

"I shall just have time to tell you the facts of the case before we get to Lee, in Kent. It seems absurdly simple, and yet, somehow, I can get nothing to go upon. There's plenty of thread, no doubt, but I can't get the end of it in my hand. Now, I'll state the case clearly and concisely to you, Watson, and maybe you may see a spark where all is dark to me."

"Proceed, then."

"Some years ago—to be definite, in May 1884—there came to Lee a gentleman, Neville St. Clair by name, who appeared to have plenty of money. He took a large villa, laid out the grounds very nicely, and lived generally in good style. By degrees he made friends in the neighborhood, and in 1887 he married the daughter of a local brewer, by whom he has now had two children. He had no occupation, but was interested in several companies, and went into town as a rule in the morning, returning by the five fourteen from Cannon Street every night. Mr. St. Clair is now thirty-seven years of age, is a man of temperate habits, a good husband, an affectionate father, and is popular with all who know him. His whole debts at the present moment, as far as we have been able to ascertain, amount to eighty-eight pounds ten shillings, while he has two hundred twenty pounds standing to his credit in the Capital and the Counties Bank. There is no reason, therefore, to think that money troubles have been weighing upon his mind.

"Last Monday Mr. St. Clair went into town rather earlier than usual, remarking before he started that he would bring his little boy home a box of bricks. By the merest chance his wife received a telegram upon this same Monday, shortly after his departure, to the effect that a small parcel of considerable value which she had been expecting was waiting for her at the Aberdeen Shipping Company. Now if you are well up in your London, you will know that the office of the company is in Fresno Street, which branches out of Upper Swandam Lane, where you found me tonight. Mrs. St. Clair had her lunch, started for the City, did some shopping, proceeded to the company's office, got her packet, and found herself exactly at four thirty-five walking through Swandam Lane on her way back to the station. Have you followed me so far?"

"It is very clear."

"Mrs. St. Clair walked slowly, glancing about in the hope of see-ing a cab, as she did not like the neighborhood in which she found herself. Suddenly she heard an ejaculation or cry, and was struck cold to see her husband looking down at her from a second-floor window. He waved his hands frantically to her, then vanished from the window so suddenly that it seemed he had been plucked back by some irresistible force. One singular point which struck her quick feminine eye was that, although he wore the dark coat he had started to town in, he had on neither collar nor necktie.

"Convinced that something was amiss with him, she rushed down the steps—for the house was none other than the opium den in which you found me tonight—and, running through the front room, she attempted to ascend the stairs which led to the second floor. At the foot of the stairs, however, she met this lascar scoun-drel, of whom I have spoken, who thrust her back, and pushed her out into the street. Filled with the most maddening doubts and fears, she rushed down the lane, and, by rare good fortune, met, in Fresno Street, a number of constables with an inspector, all on their way to their beat. The inspector and two men accompanied her back, and, in spite of the resistance of the proprietor, they made their way to the room in which Mr. St. Clair had been seen. There was no sign of him there. In fact, in the whole of that floor there was no one, save a crippled wretch of hideous aspect, who, it seems, made his home there. Both he and the lascar swore that no one else had been in the front room during that afternoon. So determined was their denial that the inspector had almost come to believe that Mrs. St. Clair had been deluded when, with a cry, she sprang at a box which lay upon the table, and tore the lid from it. Out fell a cascade of children's bricks. It was the toy which her husband had promised to bring home.

"This discovery, and the evident confusion which the cripple showed, made the inspector realize that the matter was serious. The rooms were carefully examined, and results all pointed to an abominable crime. The front room was plainly furnished as a sit-ting room, and led into a small bedroom, which looked out upon the back of one of the wharves. Between the wharf and the bedroom window is a narrow strip, which is dry at low tide, but is covered at high tide with at least four and a half feet of water. The bedroom window was a broad one, and opened from below. On examination traces of blood were to be seen upon the window-sill, and several scattered drops were visible upon the floor of the bedroom. Thrust away behind a curtain in the front room were all the clothes of Mr. Neville St. Clair, with the exception of his coat. There were no other traces of him. Out of the window he must apparently have gone, for no other exit could be discovered, and the ominous bloodstains upon the sill gave little promise that he could save himself by swimming, for the tide was at its very highest at the moment of the tragedy.

"And now as to the villains who seemed to be immediately implicated in the matter. Since the lascar was known by Mrs. St. Clair's story to have been at the foot of the stair within a few seconds of her husband's appearance at the window, he could hardly have been more than an accessory to the crime. He protested that he had no knowledge as to his lodger's doings, and that he could not account for the presence of the missing gentleman's clothes.

"Now for the sinister cripple who lives upon the second floor of the opium den. His name is Hugh Boone, and his hideous face is familiar to every man who goes much to the City. He is a professional beggar, though in order to avoid the police regulations he pretends to a small trade in matches. Upon the left-hand side of Threadneedle Street there is, as you may have remarked, a small angle in the wall. Here the creature takes his daily seat, cross-legged, with his tiny stock of matches on his lap, and as he is a piteous spectacle a small rain of charity descends into the greasy leather cap which lies upon the pavement before him. I have watched this fellow more than once, and I have been surprised at the harvest he has reaped in a short time. His appearance, you see, is so remarkable that no one can pass him without observing him. A shock of orange hair; a pale face disfigured by a horrible scar, which, by its contraction, has turned up the outer edge of his upper lip; a bulldog chin; and very penetrating dark eyes, which present a singular contrast to the color of his hair, all mark him out from the common crowd of mendicants; and so, too, does his wit, for he is ever ready with a reply to any piece of chaff which may be thrown at him by the passersby. This is the man whom we now learn to have been the last human being whose eyes rested upon Neville St. Clair."

"But a cripple!" said I. "What could he have done single-handed against a man in the prime of life?"

"He is a cripple in that he walks with a limp; but, in other respects, he appears to be powerful and well nurtured. Surely your medical experience would tell you that weakness in one limb is often compensated for by exceptional strength in the others."

"Pray continue your narrative."

"Mrs. St. Clair had fainted at the sight of the blood upon the window, and she was escorted home in a cab by the police. Inspector Barton, who had charge of the case, made a very careful examination of the premises, but without finding anything which threw any light upon the matter. Boone was searched, without anything being found which could incriminate him. There were, it is true, some bloodstains upon his right shirt sleeve, but he pointed to his ring finger, which had been cut near the nail, and explained that the bleeding came from there, adding that he had been to the window not long before, and that the stains which had been observed there came doubtless from the same source. He denied having ever seen Mr. St. Clair, and swore that the presence of the clothes in his room was as much a mystery to him as to the police. As to Mrs. St. Clair's assertion that she had seen her husband at the window, he declared that she must have been either mad or dreaming. He was removed, loudly protesting, to the police station, while the inspector remained upon the premises in the hope that the ebbing tide might afford some fresh clue.

"And it did, though they hardly found upon the mudbank what they had feared to find. It was Neville St. Clair's coat, and not Neville St. Clair, which lay uncovered as the tide receded. And what do you think they found in the pockets?"

"I cannot imagine."

"No, I don't think you will guess. Every pocket stuffed with pennies and halfpennies—four hundred and twenty-one pennies, and two hundred and seventy halfpennies. It was no wonder that the coat had not been swept away by the tide. But a human body is a different matter. There is a fierce eddy between the wharf and the house. It seemed likely that the weighted coat had remained when the stripped body had been sucked away into the river."

"But I understand that all the other clothes were found in the room. Would the body be dressed in a coat alone?"

"No, sir, but suppose that this man Boone had thrust Neville St. Clair through the window. What would he do then? It would of course instantly strike him that he must get rid of the telltale garments. He would seize the coat then, and be in the act of throwing it out when it would occur to him that it would float and not sink. He has little time, for he had heard the scuffle downstairs when the wife tried to force her way up. He rushes to some secret hoard, where he has accumulated the fruits of his beggary, and he stuffs all the coins upon which he can lay his hands into the pockets to make sure of the coat's sinking. He throws it out, and would have done the same with the other garments had not he heard the rush of steps below, and only just had time to close the window when the police appeared."

"It certainly sounds feasible."

"Well, we will take it as a working hypothesis for want of a better. Boone, as I have told you, was taken to the station, but it could not be shown that there had ever before been anything against him. He had for years been known as a professional beggar, but his life appeared to have been a quiet and innocent one. And there the matter stands at present."

Whilst Sherlock Holmes had been detailing this singular series of events we had been whirling through the outskirts of the great town until the last straggling houses had been left behind, and now we drove through two scattered villages, where a few lights still glimmered in the windows.

"We are on the outskirts of Lee," said my companion. "See that light among the trees? That is Mrs. St. Clair's home, and beside that lamp sits a woman whose anxious ears have already, I have little doubt, caught the clink of our horse's hoofs. I hate to meet her, Watson, when I have no news of her husband. Here we are. Whoa, there, whoa!"

We had pulled up in front of a large villa which stood within its own grounds. A stableboy had run out to the horse's head, and, springing down, I followed Holmes up the gravel drive which led to the house. As we approached, the door flew open, and a little blond woman stood in the opening, clad in some sort of light mousseline de soie, with a touch of fluffy pink chiffon at her neck and wrists. She stood outlined against the flood of light, one hand upon the door, one half-raised in eagerness.

"Well?" she cried. "Well?" And then, seeing that there were two of us, she gave a cry of hope which sank into a groan as she saw that my companion shook his head and shrugged.

"No good news?"

"None."

"No bad?"

"No."

"Thank God for that. But come in. You must be weary."

"This is my friend, Dr. Watson. He has been of most vital use to me in several of my cases."

"I am delighted to see you," said she, pressing my hand warmly.

"My dear madam," said I, "if I can be of any assistance, either to you or to my friend here, I shall be indeed happy."

"Now, Mr. Holmes," said the lady as we entered a well-lit dining room where a cold supper had been laid out, "I should very much like to ask you one or two plain questions, to which I beg that you will give plain answers."

"Certainly, madam."

"Do not trouble about my feelings. I am not hysterical, nor given to fainting. I simply wish to hear your real opinion. In your heart of hearts, do you think that Neville is alive?"

Sherlock Holmes seemed to be embarrassed by the question.

"Frankly now!" she said, standing upon the rug, and looking keenly down at him, as he leaned back in a basket chair.

"Frankly, then, madam, I do not."

"You think that he is dead?"

"I do."

"And on what day did he meet his death?"

"On Monday."

"Then perhaps, Mr. Holmes, you will be good enough to explain how it is that I have received this letter from him today?" She stood smiling, holding up a little slip of paper.

Holmes sprang out of his chair as if he had been galvanized. "What!" he roared. He snatched the letter from her in his eagerness, and smoothing it out upon the table, he drew over the lamp, and examined it intently. I stood and gazed at it over his shoulder. The envelope was stamped with the Gravesend postmark, and with the date of that very day, or rather of the day before, for it was after midnight.

"Coarse writing!" murmured Holmes. "Surely this is not your husband's writing, madam."

"No, but the letter is."

"I perceive also that whoever addressed the envelope had to go and inquire as to the address."

"How can you tell that?"

"The name, you see, is in black ink, which has dried itself. The rest is of the grayish color which shows that blotting paper has been used. If it had been written straight off, and then blotted, none would be of a deep black shade. This man has written the name, and there has then been a pause before he wrote the address, which can only mean that he was not familiar with it. It is a trifle, but there is nothing so important as trifles. Let us now see the letter! Ha! There has been an enclosure!"

"Yes, there was a ring. His signet ring."

"And you are sure that this is your husband's hand?"

"His hand when he wrote hurriedly. It is very unlike his usual writing, and yet I know it well."

Dearest,
    Do not be frightened. All will come well. There is a huge error which it may take some little time to rectify. Wait in patience.
                                Neville

"Written in pencil upon a flyleaf of a book, octavo size, no watermark. Posted today in Gravesend by a man with a dirty thumb. Well, Mrs. St. Clair, the clouds lighten, though I should not venture to say that the danger is over."

"But he must be alive, Mr. Holmes."

"Unless this is a clever forgery to put us on the wrong scent. The ring proves nothing. It may have been taken from him."

"No, no. It is his very own writing!"

"Very well. It may, however, have been written on Monday, and only posted today."

"That is possible."

"If so, much may have happened between."

"Oh, you must not discourage me, Mr. Holmes. I know that all is well with him. There is so keen a sympathy between us that I should know if evil came upon him. On the very day that I saw him last he cut himself in the bedroom, and yet I in the dining room rushed upstairs instantly with the utmost certainty that something had happened. Do you think that I would respond to such a trifle, and yet be ignorant of his death?"

"I have seen too much not to know that the impression of a

woman may be more valuable than the conclusion of an analytical reasoner. And in this letter you certainly have a strong piece of evidence to corroborate your view. But if your husband is alive and able to write letters, why should he remain away from you?"

"I cannot imagine. It is unthinkable."

"And on Monday you were surprised to see him in Swandam Lane?"

"Very much so."

"Was the window open?"

"Yes."

"You thought he called to you for help?"

"Yes. He waved his hands."

"But it might have been a cry of surprise. Astonishment at the unexpected sight of you might cause him to throw up his hands."

"It is possible."

"And you thought he was pulled back."

"He disappeared so suddenly."

"He might have leaped back. You did not see anyone else in the room?"

"No, but this horrible man confessed to having been there, and the lascar was at the foot of the stairs."

"Quite so. Had your husband ever spoken of Swandam Lane or ever shown any signs of having taken opium?"

"Never."

"Thank you, Mrs. St. Clair. Those are the points about which I wished to be absolutely clear. We shall now have a little supper and then retire, for we may have a very busy day tomorrow."

A LARGE AND COMFORTABLE double-bedded room had been placed at our disposal, and I was quickly between the sheets, for I was weary after my night of adventure. Sherlock Holmes was a man, however, who when he had an unsolved problem upon his mind would go for days without rest, turning it over, rearranging his facts, until he had either fathomed it, or convinced himself that his data was insufficient.

It was soon evident to me that Holmes was now preparing for

an all-night sitting. He took off his coat and waistcoat, put on a large blue dressing gown, and then wandered about the room collecting pillows from his bed, and cushions from the sofa and armchairs. With these he constructed a sort of Eastern divan, upon which he perched himself cross-legged, with an ounce of shag tobacco and a box of matches laid out in front of him. In the dim light of the lamp I saw him sitting there, an old briar pipe between his lips, his eyes fixed vacantly upon the corner of the ceiling, the blue smoke curling up from him, silent, motionless, with the light shining upon his strong-set aquiline features.

So he sat as I dropped off to sleep, and so he sat when a sudden ejaculation caused me to wake up, and I found the sun shining into the apartment. The pipe was still between his lips, the smoke still curled upwards, and the room was full of a dense tobacco haze, but nothing remained of the heap of shag which I had seen upon the previous night.

"Awake, Watson?" he asked.

"Yes."

"Game for a morning drive?"

"Certainly."

"Then dress. No one is stirring yet, but I know where the stableboy sleeps, and we shall soon have the trap out." He chuckled to himself as he spoke, and his eyes twinkled.

As I dressed I glanced at my watch. It was no wonder that no one was stirring. It was twenty-five minutes past four. I had hardly finished when Holmes returned with the news that the boy was putting in the horse.

"I want to test a little theory of mine," said he, pulling on his boots. "I think that you are in the presence of one of the most absolute fools in Europe. I deserve to be kicked from here to Charing Cross. But I think I have the key of the affair now."

"And where is it?" I asked, smiling.

"In the bathroom," he answered. "Oh, I am not joking," he continued, seeing my look of incredulity. "I have just been there and taken it out, and I have got it in this Gladstone bag. Come on, my boy, and we shall see whether it will fit the lock."

We made our way downstairs and out into the bright morning sunshine. In the road stood our horse and trap, with the half-clad stableboy waiting at the head. We both sprang in, and away we dashed down the London road. A few country carts were stirring, bearing in vegetables to the metropolis, but the villas on either side were silent and lifeless.

"I have been as blind as a mole," said Holmes, flicking the horse on into a gallop, "but it is better to learn wisdom late, than never to learn it at all."

As we drove into town, the earliest risers were just beginning to look sleepily from their windows. Passing down the Waterloo Bridge Road we crossed over the river, and dashing up Wellington Street wheeled sharply to the right, and found ourselves in Bow Street. Sherlock Holmes was well-known to the Force, and the two constables at the door saluted him. One of them held the horse's head while the other led us in.

"Ah, Bradstreet, how are you?" A tall, stout official had come down the stone-flagged passage, in a peaked cap and frogged jacket. "I wish to have a word with you, Bradstreet."

"Certainly, Mr. Holmes. Step into my room here."

It was a small officelike room, with a huge ledger upon the table, and a telephone projecting from the wall. The inspector sat down at his desk. "What can I do for you, Mr. Holmes?"

"I called about that beggarman, Boone. You have him here?"

"Yes. In the cells. He was remanded for further inquiries."

"Is he quiet?"

"Oh, he gives no trouble. But he is a dirty scoundrel. It is all we can do to make him wash his hands, and his face is as black as a tinker's."

"I should like to see him very much."

"That is easily done. Come this way, if you please. You can leave your bag."

"No, I think I'll take it."

"Very good." He led us down a passage, opened a barred door, and brought us to a whitewashed corridor with a line of doors on each side.

"The third on the right is his," said the inspector. "Here it is!" He quietly shot back a panel in the upper part of the door, and glanced through. "He is asleep," said he.

We both put our eyes to the grating. The prisoner lay with his face towards us, in a very deep sleep. He was coarsely clad as became his calling, with a colored shirt protruding through the rent in his tattered coat. He was, as the inspector had said, extremely dirty, but the grime which covered his face could not conceal its repulsive ugliness. An old scar had turned up one side of the upper lip, so that three teeth were exposed in a perpetual snarl. A shock of bright red hair grew low over his forehead.

"He's a beauty, isn't he?" said the inspector.

"He certainly needs a wash," remarked Holmes. "I had an idea that he might, and I took the liberty of bringing the tools with me." He opened his Gladstone bag as he spoke, and took out, to my astonishment, a very large bath sponge.

"He! He! You are a funny one," chuckled the inspector.

"Now, if you will have the goodness to open that door very quietly, we will soon make him cut a more respectable figure."

"Well, I don't know why not," said the inspector. "He doesn't look a credit to the Bow Street cells, does he?" He slipped the key into the lock, and we all very quietly entered the cell.

Holmes stooped to the water jug, moistened his sponge, and then rubbed it twice vigorously across and down the prisoner's face. "Let me introduce you," he shouted, "to Mr. Neville St. Clair."

Never in my life have I seen such a sight. The man's face peeled off under the sponge like the bark from a tree. Gone was the coarse brown tint! Gone, too, the horrid scar which had seamed it across, and the twisted lip which had given the repulsive sneer to the face! A twitch brought away the tangled red hair, and there, sitting up in his bed, was a pale, sad-faced, refined-looking man, black-haired and smooth-skinned, rubbing his eyes, and staring about him with sleepy bewilderment. Then realizing the exposure, he broke into a scream, and threw himself down with his face to the pillow.

"Great heaven!" cried the inspector. "It is, indeed, the missing man. I know him from the photograph."

The prisoner turned with the reckless air of a man who abandons himself to his destiny. "Be it so," said he. "And pray what am I charged with?"

"With making away with Mr. Neville St.— Oh, come, you can't be charged with that, unless they make a case of attempted suicide of it," said the inspector, with a grin. "Well, I have been twenty-seven years in the Force, but this takes the cake."

"If I am Neville St. Clair, then it is obvious that no crime has been committed, and, therefore, I am illegally detained."

"No crime, but a very great error has been committed," said Holmes. "You would have done better to have trusted your wife."

"It was not the wife, it was the children," groaned the prisoner. "God help me, I would not have them ashamed of their father. My God! What an exposure! What can I do?"

Sherlock Holmes sat down beside him on the couch, and patted him kindly on the shoulder. "If you leave it to a court of law to clear up the matter," said he, "you can hardly avoid publicity. On the other hand, if you convince the police authorities that there is no possible case against you, I do not know that there is any reason that the details should find their way into the papers. Inspector Bradstreet would, I am sure, make notes upon anything which you might tell us, and submit them to the proper authorities. The case would then never go into court."

"God bless you!" cried the prisoner passionately. "I would have endured imprisonment, aye, even execution, rather than have left my miserable secret as a family blot to my children.

"You are the first who have ever heard my story. My father was a schoolmaster in Chesterfield, where I received an excellent education. I traveled in my youth, took to the stage, and finally became a reporter on an evening paper in London. One day my editor wished to have a series of articles upon begging in the metropolis, and I volunteered to supply them. There was the point from which all my adventures started. It was only by trying begging as an amateur that I could get the facts upon which to base my articles.

When an actor, I had learned all the secrets of making up. I took advantage now of my attainments. I painted my face, and to make myself as pitiable as possible I made a good scar and fixed one side of my lip in a twist by the aid of a small slip of flesh-colored plaster. Then with a red head of hair, and an appropriate dress, I took my station in the busiest part of the City, ostensibly as a match seller, but really as a beggar. For seven hours I plied my trade, and when I returned home in the evening I found, to my surprise, that I had received no less than twenty-six shillings and fourpence.

"I wrote my articles, and thought little more of the matter until, some time later, I backed a bill for a friend, and had a writ served upon me for twenty-five pounds. I was at my wits' end where to get the money, but a sudden idea came to me. I begged a fortnight's grace from the creditor, asked for a holiday from my employers, and spent the time in begging in the City under my disguise. In ten days I had the money, and had paid the debt.

"Well, you can imagine how hard it was to settle down to arduous work at two pounds a week, when I knew that I could earn as much in a day by smearing my face with a little paint, laying my cap on the ground, and sitting still. It was a long fight between my pride and the money, but the dollars won at last, and I threw up reporting, and sat day after day in the corner which I had first chosen, inspiring pity by my ghastly face and filling my pockets with coppers.

"Only one man knew my secret. He was the keeper of a low den in which I used to lodge in Swandam Lane, where I could every morning emerge as a squalid beggar, and in the evenings transform myself into a well-dressed man-about-town. This fellow, a lascar, was well paid by me for his rooms, so that I knew that my secret was safe in his possession.

"Well, soon I was saving considerable sums of money. I do not mean that any beggar in the streets of London could earn seven hundred pounds a year—which is less than my average takings—but I had exceptional advantages in my power of making up, and also in a facility of repartee, which made me a recognized character in the City. As I grew richer I grew more ambitious, took a house in the country, and eventually married, without anyone having a suspicion as to my real occupation. My dear wife knew that I had business in the City. She little knew what.

"Last Monday I had finished for the day, and was dressing in my room above the opium den, when I looked out of the window, and saw, to my horror, that my wife was standing in the street, with her eyes fixed full upon me. I gave a cry of surprise, threw up my arms to cover my face, and rushing to my confidant, the lascar, entreated him to prevent anyone from coming up to me. I heard her voice downstairs, but I knew that she could not ascend. Swiftly I threw off my clothes, pulled on those of a beggar, and put on my pigments and wig. Even a wife's eyes could not pierce so complete a disguise. But then it occurred to me that there might be a search in the room and that the clothes might betray me. I threw open the window, reopening by my violence a small cut which I had inflicted upon myself in the bedroom that morning. Then I seized my coat, which was weighted by the coppers which I had just transferred to it from the leather bag in which I carried my takings. I hurled it out of the window, and it disappeared into the Thames. The other clothes would have followed, but at that moment there was a rush of constables up the stairs, and a few minutes afterwards I found, rather, I confess, to my relief, that instead of being identified as Mr. Neville St. Clair, I was arrested as his murderer.

"I do not know that there is anything else for me to explain. I was determined to preserve my disguise as long as possible, and hence my preference for a dirty face. Knowing that my wife would be terribly anxious, I confided my ring to the lascar at a moment when no constable was watching me, together with a hurried scrawl, telling her that she had no cause to fear."

"That note only reached her yesterday," said Holmes.

"Good God! What a week she must have spent."

"The police have watched this lascar," said Inspector Bradstreet, "and I can quite understand that he might find it difficult to post a letter unobserved."

"That was it," said Holmes, nodding approvingly, "I have no doubt of it. But have you never been prosecuted for begging?"

"Many times; but what was a fine to me?"

"It must stop here, however," said Bradstreet. "If the police are to hush this up, there must be no more of Hugh Boone."

"I swear it by the most solemn oaths which a man can take."

"In that case I think that no further steps may be taken. But if you are found again, then all must come out. I am sure, Mr. Holmes, that we are much indebted to you for having cleared the matter up. I wish I knew how you reach your results."

"I reached this one," said my friend, "by sitting upon five pillows and consuming an ounce of shag. I think, Watson, that if we drive to Baker Street we shall just be in time for breakfast."

I CALLED UPON MY FRIEND, Sherlock Holmes, one day in the autumn of 1890, and found him in deep conversation with a stout, florid-faced, elderly gentleman with fiery red hair. With an apology for my intrusion, I was about to withdraw, when Holmes pulled me abruptly into the room, and closed the door behind me.

"You could not possibly have come at a better time, my dear Watson," he said cordially. "This gentleman, Mr. Wilson, has been my partner in many of my most successful cases, and I have no doubt that he will be of the utmost use to me in yours also."

The stout gentleman half rose from his chair, and gave a bob of greeting, with a quick little questioning glance from his small, fat-encircled eyes.

"Try the settee," said Holmes, relapsing into his armchair, and putting his fingertips together, as was his custom when in judicial moods. "I know, my dear Watson, that you share my love of all that is bizarre and outside the humdrum routine of everyday life. You will remember that I remarked the other day, that for strange effects and extraordinary combinations we must go to life itself, which is always far more daring than any effort of the imagination. Now, Mr. Jabez Wilson here has been good enough to call upon me this morning, and to begin a narrative which promises to be one of the most singular which I have listened to for some time. Perhaps, Mr. Wilson, you would have the kindness to recommence your narrative."

The portly client puffed out his chest with an appearance of some little pride, and pulled a dirty and wrinkled newspaper from the inside pocket of his greatcoat. As he glanced down the advertisement column, with his head thrust forward, and the paper flattened out upon his knee, I took a good look at the man, and endeavored after the fashion of my companion to read the indications which might be presented by his dress or appearance.

I did not gain much, however, by my inspection. Our visitor bore every mark of being a commonplace British tradesman, obese, pompous, and slow. He wore rather baggy gray shepherd's-check trousers, a not overclean black frock coat, unbuttoned in the front, and a drab waistcoat with a heavy, brassy Albert chain, and a square, pierced bit of metal dangling down as an ornament. A frayed top hat, and a faded brown overcoat with a wrinkled velvet collar lay upon a chair beside him. Look as I would, there was nothing remarkable about the man save his blazing red hair.

Sherlock Holmes's quick eye took in my occupation and he shook his head with a smile as he noticed my questioning glances. "Beyond the obvious facts that he has at some time done manual labor, that he has been in China, and that he has done a considerable amount of writing lately, I can deduce nothing else."

Mr. Jabez Wilson started up in his chair. "How, in the name of good fortune, did you know all that, Mr. Holmes?" he asked. "How did you know, for example, that I did manual labor? It's as true as gospel, and I began as a ship's carpenter."

"Your right hand is quite a size larger than your left. You have worked with it, and the muscles are more developed."

"Well, then, the writing?"

"What else can be indicated by that right cuff so very shiny for five inches, and the left sleeve with the smooth patch near the elbow where you rest it upon the desk."

"Well, but China?"

"The fish which you have tattooed immediately above your right wrist could only have been done in China. I have made a small study of tattoo marks, and have even contributed to the literature of the subject. That trick of staining the fishes' scales a delicate pink is quite peculiar to China. In addition, I see a Chinese coin hanging from your watch chain."

Mr. Jabez Wilson laughed heavily. "Well, I never!" said he. "I thought at first you had done something clever, but I see that there was nothing in it after all."

"I think, Watson," said Holmes, "that I made a mistake in explaining. My poor little reputation will suffer shipwreck if I am so candid. Can you not find the advertisement, Mr. Wilson?"

"Yes, I have got it now," he answered, with his thick, red finger planted halfway down the column. "Here it is. This is what began it all. You just read it for yourself, sir."

I took the paper from him and read as follows:

To THE RED-HEADED LEAGUE: On account of the bequest of the late Ezekiah Hopkins, of Lebanon, Pa., U.S.A., there is now another vacancy open which entitles a member of the League to a salary of four pounds a week for purely nominal services. All red-headed men who are sound in body and mind, and above the age of twenty-one years, are eligible. Apply in person on Monday, at eleven o'clock, to Duncan Ross, at the offices of the League, 7 Pope's Court, Fleet Street.

"What on earth does this mean?" I ejaculated, after I had twice read over the extraordinary announcement.

Holmes chuckled, and wriggled in his chair, as was his habit when in high spirits. "It is a little off the beaten track, isn't it?" said he. "And now, Mr. Wilson, off you go at scratch, and tell us all about yourself, your household, and the effect which this advertisement had upon your fortunes. You will first make a note, Doctor, of the paper and the date."

"It is the *Morning Chronicle* of August 7, 1890. Just about two months ago."

"Very good. Now, Mr. Wilson?"

"Well, it is just as I have been telling you, Mr. Holmes," said Jabez Wilson, mopping his forehead. "I have a pawnbroker's business at Saxe-Coburg Square, near the City. It's not a very large affair, and of late years it has not done more than just give me a living. I used to be able to keep two assistants, but now I only keep one; and I would have a job to pay him, but that he is willing to come for half wages, so as to learn the business."

"What is the name of this obliging youth?" asked Holmes.

"His name is Vincent Spaulding, and I should not wish a smarter assistant. I know he could earn twice what I give him. But, if he is satisfied, why should I put ideas in his head?"

"Why, indeed? You seem most fortunate. I don't know that your assistant is not as remarkable as your advertisement."

"Oh, he has his faults, too," said Mr. Wilson. "Never was such a fellow for photography. Snapping away with a camera when he ought to be improving his mind, and then diving down into the cellar like a rabbit into its hole to develop his pictures; but on the whole, he's a good worker. He and a girl of fourteen, who does a bit of simple cooking, and keeps the place clean—that's all I have in the house, for I am a widower, and never had any family. We live very quietly, sir, the three of us; and the first thing that put us out was that advertisement. Spaulding, he came down into the office eight weeks ago with this very paper in his hand, and he says: 'I wish to the Lord, Mr. Wilson, that I was a red-headed man.'

"'Why that?' I asks.

"'Why,' says he, 'here's a vacancy on the Red-headed League. It's worth quite a little fortune to any man who gets it.'

"'Why, what is it, then?' I asked. You see, Mr. Holmes, I am a very stay-at-home man, and, as my business came to me instead of my having to go to it, I was often weeks on end without putting my foot over the doormat. In that way I didn't know much of what was going on outside, and I was always glad of a bit of news.

"'Have you never heard of the Red-headed League?' he asked, with his eyes wide.

"'Never.'

"'Why, I wonder at that, for you are eligible yourself for one of the vacancies.'

"'And what are they worth?' I asked.

"'Oh, merely a couple of hundred a year, but the work is slight, and it need not interfere with one's other occupations.'

"Well, you can easily think how that made me prick up my ears. 'Tell me all about it,' said I.

"'Well,' said he, showing me the advertisement, 'there is the address where you should apply for particulars. As far as I can make out, the League was founded by an American millionaire, Ezekiah Hopkins, who was very peculiar in his ways. He was himself red-headed, and he had a great sympathy for all red-headed men; so, when he died, he left his enormous fortune in the hands of trustees, with instructions to apply the interest to the providing of easy berths to men whose hair is of that color.'

"'But,' said I, 'there would be millions of red-headed men who would apply.'

"'Not so many as you might think,' he answered. 'You see, it is really confined to Londoners, and to grown men. This American had started from London when he was young, and he wanted to do the old town a good turn. Then, again, I have heard it is no use applying if your hair is light red, or dark red, or anything but real, bright, blazing, fiery red.'

"Now, gentlemen, as you may see for yourselves, my hair is of a very full and rich tint, so it seemed to me that I stood as good a chance as any man that I had ever met. So I ordered Vincent Spaulding to put up the shutters for the day, and to come right away with me. He was very willing to have a holiday, so we started off to the address that was given in the advertisement.

"I never hope to see such a sight as that again, Mr. Holmes. From north, south, east, and west every man who had a shade of red in his hair had tramped into the City to answer the advertisement. Every shade of the color they were—straw, lemon, orange, brick, Irish-setter, liver, clay; but there were not many who had the real vivid flame-colored tint. When I saw how many were waiting, I would have given it up in despair; but Spaulding would not hear of it. He pushed and pulled and butted until he got me through the crowd, and right up to the steps which led to the office. There was a double stream upon the stair, some going up in hope, and some coming back dejected; but we wedged in as well as we could, and soon found ourselves in the office."

Mr. Wilson paused and refreshed his memory with a huge pinch of snuff. "Pray continue," said Holmes.

"There was nothing in the office but a couple of wooden chairs and a deal table, behind which sat a small man, with a head that was even redder than mine. He said a few words to each candidate as he came up, and then he always managed to find some fault in them which would disqualify them. However, when our turn came, the little man was more favorable to me than to any of the others, and he closed the door as we entered, so that he might have a private word with us.

"'This is Mr. Jabez Wilson,' said my assistant, 'and he is willing to fill a vacancy in the League.'

"'And he is admirably suited for it,' the other answered. 'I cannot recall when I have seen anything so fine.' He took a step backwards, cocked his head on one side, and gazed at my hair until I felt quite bashful. Then suddenly he plunged forward, wrung my hand, and congratulated me warmly on my success.

"'It would be injustice to hesitate,' said he. 'You will, however, I am sure, excuse me for taking an obvious precaution.' With that he seized my hair in both his hands, and tugged until I yelled with the pain. 'There is water in your eyes,' said he, as he released me. 'I perceive that all is as it should be. But we have to be careful, for we have twice been deceived by wigs and once by paint.' He stepped over to the window, and shouted through it that the vacancy was filled. A groan of disappointment came up from below, and the folk all trooped away in different directions.

"'My name,' said he, 'is Mr. Duncan Ross, and I am myself one of the pensioners upon the fund left by our noble benefactor. When can you enter upon your new duties, Mr. Wilson?'

"'Well, it is awkward, for I have a business,' said I.

"'Oh, never mind about that, Mr. Wilson!' said Vincent Spaulding. 'I shall be able to look after that for you.'

"'What would be the hours?' I asked.

"'Ten to two.'

"Now a pawnbroker's business is mostly done of an evening, Mr. Holmes, especially Thursday and Friday evening, which is just before payday; so it would suit me very well to earn a little in the mornings. Besides, I knew that my assistant was a good man, and that he would see to anything that turned up.

"'That would suit me very well,' said I. 'And the pay?'

"'Four pounds a week. You have to be in the office, or at least in the building, the whole time. If you leave, you forfeit your position. The will is very clear upon that point, and no excuse will avail.'

"'I should not think of leaving,' said I. 'And the work?'

"'Is to copy the *Encyclopaedia Britannica*. There is the first volume of it in that cupboard. You must find your own ink, pens, and blotting paper, but we provide this table and chair. Will you be ready tomorrow?'

"'Certainly,' I answered.

"'Then, good-by, Mr. Jabez Wilson, and let me congratulate you once more on the important position which you have been fortunate enough to gain.' He bowed me out of the room, and I went home with my assistant, very pleased at my good fortune.

"Well, I thought over the matter all day, and by evening I had quite persuaded myself that the whole affair must be some great hoax, though what its object might be I could not imagine. It seemed altogether past belief that anyone could make such a will, or that they would pay such a sum for doing anything so simple as copying out the *Encyclopaedia Britannica*. However, in the morning I determined to have a look at it anyhow, so, with a bottle of ink, a quill pen, and seven sheets of foolscap paper, I started off for Pope's Court.

"Well, to my surprise and delight everything was as right as possible, and Mr. Duncan Ross was there to see that I got fairly to work. He started me off upon the letter A, and then he left me; but he would drop in from time to time to see that all was right. At two o'clock he bade me good day, complimented me upon the amount I had written, and locked the door of the office after me.

"This went on day after day, Mr. Holmes, and on Saturday the manager planked down four golden sovereigns for my week's work. It was the same next week, and the week after. By degrees Mr. Ross took to coming in only once of a morning, and then, after a time, he did not come in at all. Still, I never dared to leave the room, for I was not sure when he might come, and the billet was such a good one that I would not risk the loss of it.

"Eight weeks passed away like this, and I had written about Abbots, and Archery, and Architecture, and Armour, and Attica, and hoped with diligence that I might get on to the B's before very long. It cost me something in foolscap, and I had pretty nearly filled a shelf with my writings. And then suddenly the whole business came to an end."

"To an end?"

"Yes, sir. This morning I went to my work as usual at ten o'clock, but the door was locked, with a little square of cardboard hammered onto the middle of the panel with a tack. Here it is." He held up a piece of white cardboard, about the size of a sheet of notepaper. It read in this fashion:

THE RED-HEADED LEAGUE IS DISSOLVED: OCT. 9, 1890

Sherlock Holmes and I surveyed this curt announcement and the rueful face behind it, until the comical side of the affair so completely overtopped every other consideration that we both burst out into a roar of laughter.

"I cannot see that there is anything very funny," cried our client, flushing up to the roots of his flaming head. "If you can do nothing better than laugh at me, I can go elsewhere."

"No, no," cried Holmes, shoving him back into the chair from which he had half risen. "I wouldn't miss your case for the world. It is refreshingly unusual. But there is, if you will excuse me saying so, something just a little funny about it. Pray what did you do when you found the card upon the door?"

"I called at the offices round, but none of them seemed to know anything about it. Finally, I went to the landlord, who is an accountant living on the ground floor, and I asked him if he could tell me what had become of the Red-headed League. He said that he had never heard of any such body. Then I asked him who Mr. Duncan Ross was. He answered that the name was new to him.

"'Well,' said I, 'the gentleman at Number 4.'

"'Oh,' said he, 'his name was William Morris. He was a solicitor, and was using my room as a temporary convenience until his new premises were ready. He moved yesterday to his new offices at 17 King Edward Street, near St. Paul's.'

"I started off, Mr. Holmes, but when I got to that address it was a manufactory of artificial kneecaps, and no one in it had ever heard of either Mr. William Morris or Mr. Duncan Ross."

"And what did you do then?" asked Holmes.

"I went home, and I asked the advice of my assistant. But he could only say that if I waited I should hear by post. But that was not quite good enough, Mr. Holmes. I did not wish to lose such a place without a struggle, so, as I had heard that you were good enough to give advice to poor folk who were in need of it, I came right away to you."

"And you did very wisely," said Holmes. "From what you have told me I think that it is possible that graver issues hang from your case than might at first sight appear."

"Grave enough!" said Mr. Jabez Wilson. "Why, I have lost four pounds a week."

"On the contrary," remarked Holmes, "you are richer by some thirty pounds, to say nothing of the minute knowledge you have gained on every subject which comes under the letter A."

"But I want to find out who they are, and what their object was in playing this prank—if it was a prank—upon me."

"We shall endeavor to clear up these points. And, first, one or two questions, Mr. Wilson. This assistant of yours who first called your attention to the advertisement—how long had he been with you?"

"About a month then."

"How did he come?"

"In answer to an advertisement."

"Was he the only applicant?"

"No, I had a dozen."

"Why did you pick him?"

"Because he was handy, and would come at half wages."

"What is he like, this Vincent Spaulding?"

"Small, stout-built, very quick in his ways, no hair on his face. Has a white splash from acid upon his forehead."

"Hum!" said Holmes, sinking back in deep thought. "And has your business been attended to in your absence?"

"Nothing to complain of, sir. There's not much to do of a morning."

"That will do, Mr. Wilson. I shall be happy to give you an opinion upon the subject in a day or two. I hope that by Monday we may come to a conclusion."

"Well, Watson," said Holmes, when our visitor had left us, "what do you make of it all?"

"I make nothing of it," I answered frankly. "It is a most mysterious business."

"As a rule," said Holmes, "the more bizarre a thing is the less mysterious it proves to be. It is your commonplace, featureless crimes which are really puzzling. But I must be prompt over this matter."

"What are you going to do then?" I asked.

"To smoke," he answered. "It is quite a three-pipe problem, and I beg you not to speak to me for fifty minutes." He curled up in his chair, with his thin knees drawn up to his hawklike nose, and there he sat with his eyes closed and his black clay pipe thrusting out like the bill of some strange bird. I had come to the conclusion that he had dropped asleep, and indeed was nodding myself, when he sprang up with the gesture of a man who had made up his mind, and put his pipe down upon the mantelpiece.

"Sarasate plays at the St. James's Hall this afternoon," he remarked. "Will you come? I am going through the City first, and we can have some lunch on the way. I observe that there is a good deal of German music on the program. It is introspective, and I want to introspect. Come along!"

I agreed, and we traveled by the Underground as far as Aldersgate; and a short walk took us to Saxe-Coburg Square, the scene of the singular story which we had listened to in the morning. It was a shabby-genteel little place, where four lines of dingy two-storied brick houses looked out into a small railed-in enclosure, where a lawn of weedy grass and a few clumps of faded laurel made a hard fight against a smoke-laden atmosphere. Three gilt balls and a board with JABEZ WILSON in white letters, upon a corner house, announced the place where our red-headed client carried on his business. Holmes stopped in front of it with his head on one side and looked it all over, with his eyes shining brightly between puckered lids. Then he walked slowly up and down the street, looking keenly at the houses. Finally he returned to the pawnbroker's, and, having thumped vigorously upon the pavement with his stick two or three times, he went up to the door and knocked. It was opened by a bright-looking, clean-shaven young fellow, who asked him to step in.

"Thank you," said Holmes. "I only wished to ask you how you would go from here to the Strand."

"Third right, fourth left," answered the assistant promptly.

"Smart fellow, that," observed Holmes as we walked away. "He is, in my judgment, the fourth smartest man in London, and for daring I am not sure that he has not a claim to be third. I have known something of him before."

"Evidently," said I, "Mr. Wilson's assistant counts for a good deal in this mystery of the Red-headed League. I am sure you inquired your way merely in order that you might see him."

"Not him—the knees of his trousers."

"And what did you see?"

"What I expected to see."

"Why did you beat the pavement?"

"My dear Doctor, this is a time for observation, not for talk. We are spies in an enemy's country. We know something of Saxe-Coburg Square. Let us now explore the paths which lie behind it."

The road in which we found ourselves as we turned round the corner from the secluded Saxe-Coburg Square presented as great a contrast to it as the front of a picture does to the back. It was one of the main arteries which convey the traffic of the City to the north and west. The roadway was blocked with the immense stream of commerce flowing in a double tide inwards and outwards, while the footpaths were black with hurrying pedestrians.

"Let me see," said Holmes, standing at the corner, and glancing along the line, "I should like to remember the order of the houses here. It is a hobby of mine to have an exact knowledge of London. There is the tobacconist, the little newspaper shop, the Coburg branch of the City and Suburban Bank, the Vegetarian Restaurant, and McFarlane's carriage-building depot. That carries us on to the other block. And now, Doctor, we've done our work, so it's time we had some play. A sandwich, and a cup of coffee, and then off to violin land, where all is sweetness and harmony, and there are no red-headed clients to vex us."

All the afternoon my friend sat in the stalls wrapped in perfect happiness, waving his long thin fingers in time to the music, while his gently smiling face and his dreamy eyes were as unlike those of Holmes the relentless, keen-witted sleuthhound as it was possible to conceive. In his singular character the extreme exactness and astuteness represented, as I have often thought, the reaction against the poetic and contemplative mood which occasionally predominated in him; and he was never so formidable as when, for days on end, he had been lounging in his armchair amid his black-letter musical scores. Then it was that the lust of the chase would suddenly come upon him, and that his brilliant reasoning power would rise to the level of intuition. When I saw him that afternoon so enwrapped in the music at St. James's Hall I felt that an evil time might be coming upon those whom he had set himself to hunt down.

"You want to go home, Doctor?" he asked, as we emerged.

"Yes, it would be as well."

"And I have business to do which will take some hours. A considerable crime is in contemplation. I have reason to believe that we shall be in time to stop it. But today being Saturday complicates matters. I shall want your help tonight at ten."

"I shall be at Baker Street at ten."

"Very well. And, I say, Doctor, there may be some little danger, so kindly put your army revolver in your pocket." He waved his hand, turned on his heel, and disappeared among the crowd.

I trust that I am not more dense than my neighbors, but I was always oppressed with a sense of my own stupidity in my dealings with Sherlock Holmes. Here I had heard what he had heard, I had seen what he had seen, and yet from his words it was evident that he saw clearly not only what had happened, but what was about to happen, while to me the whole business was still confused and grotesque.

As I drove home to my house in Kensington I thought over it all, from the extraordinary story of the red-headed copier of the *Encyclopaedia* down to the visit to Saxe-Coburg Square, and the ominous words with which Holmes had parted from me. What was this nocturnal expedition, and why should I go armed? I had the hint from Holmes that this smooth-faced pawnbroker's assistant was a formidable man—a man who might play a deep game. I tried to puzzle it out, but gave it up in despair.

It was a quarter past nine when I started from home and made my way across the Park, and so through Oxford Street to Baker Street. Two hansoms were standing at the door, and, as I entered the passage, I heard the sound of voices from above. On entering his room, I found Holmes in animated conversation with two men, one of whom I recognized as Peter Jones, the official police agent; while the other was a long, thin, sad-faced man, with a very shiny hat and oppressively respectable frock coat.

"Ha! Our party is complete," said Holmes, buttoning up his pea jacket, and taking his heavy hunting crop from the rack. "Watson, you know Mr. Jones, of Scotland Yard? Let me introduce you to Mr. Merryweather, who is to be our companion in tonight's adventure."

"We're hunting in couples again, Doctor, you see," said Jones in his consequential way. "Our friend here is a wonderful man for starting a chase. All he wants is an old dog to help him to do the running down."

"I hope a wild goose may not prove to be the end of our chase," observed Mr. Merryweather gloomily.

"You may place considerable confidence in Mr. Holmes, sir," said the police agent loftily. "He has his own little methods, which are, if he won't mind my saying so, just a little too theoretical and fantastic, but he has the makings of a detective in him.

It is not too much to say that once or twice he has been more nearly correct than the official force."

"If you say so, Mr. Jones," said the stranger, with deference. "Still, I miss my whist. It is the first Saturday night for seven-and-twenty years that I have not had my rubber of whist."

"I think you will find," said Sherlock Holmes, "that you will play for a higher stake tonight than you have ever done yet, and that the play will be more exciting. For you, Mr. Merryweather, the stake will be some thirty thousand pounds; and for you, Jones, it will be the man upon whom you wish to lay your hands."

"John Clay, the murderer, thief, smasher, and forger," said Jones. "He's a young man, Mr. Merryweather, but he is at the head of his profession, and I would rather have my bracelets on him than on any other criminal in London. He's a remarkable man, is young John Clay. His grandfather was a royal duke, and he himself has been to Eton and Oxford. His brain is as cunning as his fingers: he'll crack a crib in Scotland one week, and be raising money to build an orphanage in Cornwall the next. I've been on his track for years, and have never set eyes on him yet."

"I hope I may have the pleasure of introducing you tonight. It is past ten, however, and quite time we started. If you two will take the first hansom, Watson and I will follow in the second."

Sherlock Holmes was not very communicative during the long drive, and lay back in the cab humming the tunes which he had heard in the afternoon. We rattled through an endless labyrinth of gaslit streets until we emerged into Farringdon Street.

"This fellow Merryweather is personally interested in the matter," my friend remarked. "I thought it as well to have Jones with us also. He is not a bad fellow, though an absolute imbecile in his profession. He has one positive virtue. He is as brave as a bulldog, and as tenacious as a lobster if he gets his claws upon anyone. Here we are, and they are waiting for us."

We had reached the same crowded thoroughfare in which we had found ourselves in the morning. Our cabs were dismissed, and, following Mr. Merryweather, we passed down a narrow passage, and through a side door, which he opened for us. Within there was a small corridor, which ended in a massive iron gate. This also was opened, and led down a flight of winding stone steps, which terminated at another formidable gate. Mr. Merryweather stopped to light a lantern, and then conducted us down a dark, earth-smelling passage, and so, after opening a third door, into a huge vault or cellar, which was piled all round with crates and boxes.

"You are not very vulnerable from above," Holmes remarked, as he gazed about him.

"Nor from below," said Mr. Merryweather, striking his stick upon the flags which lined the floor. "Why, dear me, it sounds quite hollow!" he remarked, looking up in surprise.

"I must really ask you to be a little more quiet," said Holmes severely. "You have already imperiled the success of our expedition. Might I beg that you would have the goodness to sit down upon one of those boxes, and not to interfere?"

The solemn Mr. Merryweather perched himself upon a crate, with a very injured expression upon his face, while Holmes fell upon his knees upon the floor, and, with the lantern and a magnifying lens, began to examine minutely the cracks between the stones. A few seconds sufficed to satisfy him, for he sprang to his feet again, and put his glass in his pocket.

"We have at least an hour before us," he remarked, "for they can hardly take any steps until the good pawnbroker is safely in bed. Then they will not lose a minute, for the sooner they do their work the longer they will have for their escape. We are, Doctor—as no doubt you have divined—in the cellar of the City branch of one of the principal London banks. Mr. Merryweather is the chairman of directors, and he will explain to you that there are reasons why the more daring criminals of London should take a considerable interest in this cellar at present."

"It is our French gold," whispered the director. "We have had several warnings that an attempt might be made upon it."

"Your French gold?"

"Yes. We had occasion some months ago to strengthen our resources, and borrowed, for that purpose, thirty thousand napoleons from the Bank of France. It has become known that we have never unpacked the money, and that it is lying in our cellar. The crate upon which I sit contains two thousand napoleons packed between layers of lead foil. Our reserve of bullion is much larger at present than is usually kept in a single branch office, and the directors have had misgivings upon the subject."

"Which were very well justified," observed Holmes. "And now it is time that we arranged our little plans. Mr. Merryweather, we must put the screen over that lantern."

"And sit in the dark?"

"I am afraid so. I had brought a pack of cards in my pocket, and I thought you might have your game of whist after all. But I see that the enemy's preparations have gone so far that we cannot risk the presence of a light. These are daring men, and, though we shall take them at a disadvantage, they may do us some harm, unless we are careful. I shall stand behind this crate, and do you conceal yourselves behind those. Then, when I flash a light upon them, close in swiftly. If they fire, Watson, have no compunction about shooting them down."

I placed my revolver, cocked, upon the top of the wooden case behind which I crouched. Holmes shot the slide across the front of the lantern, and left us in pitch-darkness. To me, there was something depressing and subduing in the sudden gloom, and in the cold, dank air of the vault.

"They have but one retreat," whispered Holmes. "That is back through the house into Saxe-Coburg Square. I hope that you have done what I asked you, Jones?"

"An inspector and two officers are waiting at the front door."

"Then we have stopped all the holes. Now we must be silent and wait."

What a time it seemed! From comparing notes afterwards it was but an hour and a quarter, yet it appeared to me that the night must have gone, and the dawn be breaking above us. My limbs were weary and stiff, for I feared to change my position, yet my nerves were worked up to a high pitch of tension, and my hearing was so acute that I could not only hear the gentle breathing of my companions, but I could distinguish the deeper, heavier inbreath of the bulky Jones from the thin sighing note of the bank director. From my position I could look over the case in the direction of the floor. Suddenly my eyes caught a glint of light.

At first it was but a lurid spark upon the stone floor. Then it lengthened until it became a yellow line, and then, without any sound, a gash opened and a hand appeared, which felt about in the center of the little area of light. For a minute or more the hand, with its writhing fingers, protruded out of the floor. Then it was withdrawn, as suddenly as it had appeared, and all was dark again save the single lurid spark, which marked a chink between the stones.

Its disappearance, however, was but momentary. With a rending, tearing sound, one of the broad stones turned over upon its side, and left a square, gaping hole, through which streamed the light of a lantern. Over the edge there peeped a clean-cut, boyish face, which looked keenly about it, and then, with a hand on either side of the aperture, drew itself shoulder high and waist high, until one knee rested upon the edge. In another instant he stood at the side of the hole, and was hauling after him a companion, lithe and small like himself, with a pale face and a shock of very red hair.

"It's all clear," he whispered. "Have you the chisel, and the bags? Great Scott! Jump, Archie, jump, and I'll swing for it!"

Holmes had sprung out and seized the intruder by the collar. The other dived down the hole, and I heard the sound of rending cloth as Jones clutched at his coat. The light flashed upon the barrel of a revolver, but Holmes's crop came down on the man's wrist, and the pistol clinked upon the stone floor.

"It's no use, John Clay," said Holmes blandly. "You have no chance at all."

"So I see," Clay answered with the utmost coolness. "I fancy that my pal is all right, though I see you've got his coattails."

"There are three men waiting for him at the door," said Holmes.

"Oh, indeed. You seem to have done the thing very completely. I must compliment you."

"And I you," Holmes answered. "Your red-headed idea was very new and effective."

"You'll see your pal again presently," said Jones. "Just hold out while I fix the derbies."

"I beg that you will not touch me with your filthy hands," remarked our prisoner, as the handcuffs clattered upon his wrists. "You may not be aware that I have royal blood in my veins. Have the goodness also when you address me to say 'sir' and 'please.'"

"All right," said Jones, with a stare and a snicker. "Well, would you please, sir, march upstairs, where we can get a cab to carry your highness to the police station."

"That is better," said Clay serenely. He made a sweeping bow to the three of us, and walked off in the custody of the detective.

"Really, Mr. Holmes," said Mr. Merryweather, as we followed them from the cellar, "I do not know how the bank can thank you or repay you. There is no doubt that you have detected and defeated in the most complete manner a most determined attempt at bank robbery."

"I have been at some small expense over this matter, which I shall expect the bank to refund," said Holmes, "but beyond that I am amply repaid by having had an experience which is in many ways unique."

"YOU SEE, WATSON," HE EXPLAINED in the early hours of the morning, as we sat over a glass of whisky and soda in Baker Street, "it was obvious from the first that the only possible object of this rather fantastic business of the advertisement of the League, and the copying of the *Encyclopaedia*, must be to get this not overbright pawnbroker out of the way for a number of hours every day. It was a curious way of managing it, but really it would be difficult to suggest a better. The method was no doubt suggested to Clay's ingenious mind by the color of his accomplice's hair. The four pounds a week was a lure which must draw Wilson, and what was it to them, who were playing for thousands? They put in the advertisement; one rogue has the temporary office, the other incites the man to apply for it, and together they secure his absence every morning in the week. From the time that I heard of the assistant having come for half wages, it was obvious to me that he had strong motives for securing the situation."

"But how could you guess what the motive was?"

"Had there been women in the house, I should have suspected a mere vulgar intrigue. That, however, was out of the question. The man's business was a small one, and there was nothing in his house which could account for such elaborate preparations and such an expenditure as they were at. It must then be something out of the house. What could it be? I thought of the assistant's fondness for photography, and his trick of vanishing into the cellar. The cellar! That was the end of this tangled clue. Then I made inquiries as to this mysterious assistant, and found that I had to deal with one of the coolest and most daring criminals in London. He was doing something in the cellar which took many hours a day for months on end. What could it be, once more? I could think of nothing save that he was running a tunnel to some other building.

"When we visited the scene of action, I surprised you by beating upon the pavement with my stick. I was ascertaining whether the cellar stretched out in front or behind. It was not in front. Then I rang the bell, and, as I hoped, the assistant answered it. We have had some skirmishes, but we had never set eyes on each other before. I hardly looked at his face. His knees were what I wished to see. You must yourself have remarked how worn and stained they were. They spoke of those hours of burrowing. The only remaining point was what they were burrowing for. I walked round the corner, saw that the City and Suburban Bank abutted on our friend's premises, and felt that I had solved my problem. When you drove home after the concert I called upon Scotland Yard, and upon the chairman of the bank directors, with the result that you have seen."

"And how could you tell that they would make their attempt tonight?" I asked.

"Well, when they closed their League offices that was a sign that they cared no longer about Mr. Jabez Wilson's presence; in other words, that they had completed their tunnel. But it was essential that they should use it soon, as it might be discovered, or the bullion might be removed. Saturday would suit them better than any other day, as it would give them two days for their escape. For all these reasons I expected them to come tonight."

"You reasoned it out beautifully," I exclaimed in unfeigned admiration. "It is a long chain, and yet every link rings true."

"It saved me from ennui," he answered, yawning. "Alas, I already feel it closing in upon me! My life is spent in one long effort to escape from the commonplaces of existence. These little problems help me to do so."

"And you are a benefactor of the race," said I.

He shrugged his shoulders. "Well, perhaps, after all, it is of some little use," he remarked. "'*L'homme c'est rien—l'oeuvre c'est tout*,' as Gustave Flaubert wrote to George Sand."

Arthur Conan Doyle
(1859–1930)

"ON THE CONTRARY, Watson, you can see everything. You fail, however, to draw inferences from what you see." This observation—terse, irrefutable, and arrogant—is typical of Sherlock Holmes, master detective and a legend to sleuthing aficionados the world over. In fact, he is so convincing a character that fans are tempted to overlook his creator, Sir Arthur Conan Doyle, physician, social reformer, and the mastermind behind Sherlock Holmes.

Arthur Conan Doyle's life began on May 22, 1859, and from the beginning the plot was vexing. His father, Charles, was an aspiring artist laboring for Scotland's Board of Works, eking out a small living for his wife and six children. But before Doyle reached maturity, his father was ruined by alcohol, unable to hold down a job.

The family survived because of the efforts of his mother, Mary Doyle. She was from a noble family, a distant cousin of Sir Walter Scott, and encouraged Arthur's interest in historical romances and tales of knightly chivalry. To meet the family's mounting debt she took in boarders. Among them was Bryan Charles Waller, a physician who took charge of the chaotic household. His influence would help Doyle avoid the path of his father, whose ambitions were always frustrated, and opt instead for the more reliable, antiseptic calling of medicine.

Doyle began medical school in the fall of 1876 at the Royal Infirmary in Edinburgh. There he cultivated the clinical detachment and steely methods of deduction that formed Sherlock Holmes's flawless displays of reasoning. Equally important during Doyle's stint at Edinburgh was his encounter with Holmes's real-life prototype, the surgeon and clinical instructor Joseph Bell. Bell's intellect was sharp and exacting. So legendary were his feats of deduction that he was said to diagnose rare and clinically ambiguous maladies on sight, prior to getting a history from the patient, with an amphitheater of medical students watching. Doyle was enthralled by the logical skills of this remarkable man, although he did not share Bell's passion for medicine.

During the summer of 1880 on a leave from school, Doyle set out on his "first real adventure," sailing for Greenland with a whaling expedition. The following year, having graduated from medical school, he headed south of the equator as the ship's surgeon of the West African freighter *Mayumba*. But with this excursion Doyle cured himself of wanderlust, wearied by the stifling heat and bored by dreary ports.

Returning to England in June 1882, Doyle was in for more monotony scouting for patients to fill his empty consultation room. His sluggish practice gave Doyle plenty of time to try his hand at fiction. In July 1883, he published his first story, a mystery entitled "J. Habukuk Jephson's Statement."

Doyle had been married to Louise Hawkins for less than five years when, frustrated with country doctoring, he relocated to London. Once again he found himself without a steady supply of patients. "Not one single patient ever crossed the threshold of my consulting room," he would later recall. Whiling away the hours, Doyle conjured up Sherlock Holmes. The first novel to feature him was *A Study in Scarlet*, serialized by *Beeton's Christmas Annual* in December 1887.

In Holmes, Doyle had created a character that would dog him for the rest of his life. The public could not get enough of Holmes. In 1891, Sherlock Holmes was a regular feature in *The Strand* magazine, following the huge success of *The Sign of Four*. By 1893, Doyle was financially secure, retiring from medicine to devote himself to his first passion, the historical novel.

Tired of the character of Holmes, Doyle finished him off, hurling him to his death from the top of a Swiss waterfall in the clutches of his deadliest foe. But the public would not have it. Readers lobbied, dispatching angry letters to Doyle and his editors. Some formed Let's Keep Holmes Alive clubs. When his other literary efforts failed to generate the attention, and income, of Detective Holmes, Doyle finally conceded. Sherlock Holmes was restored to life in 1902, returning from the incident at Reichenbach Falls in the story *The Adventure of the Empty House*.

In the years of Holmes' absence, Doyle devoted his energies to historical research and social reform. He was a war correspondent for the *Westminster*

Gazette during Britain's battle with the Sudanese in 1887 and 1888. In 1902, he was knighted for his writing on the Boer War, collected in the volumes *The War in South Africa: Its Causes and Conduct*.

Following the death of his wife in 1906, Doyle became a champion of social reform. He lobbied aggressively to overturn the conviction of a murderer he felt had been wrongly accused. He ran for Parliament twice, and was defeated both times. He also lectured as a spokesman for divorce reform.

In 1907 Doyle married Jean Leckie, and together they pursued Doyle's long-held fascination with spiritualism. They traveled throughout Europe giving lectures and attending spiritualist congresses. Doyle worked with the escape artist and skeptic Harry Houdini publicly investigating the claims of several well-known mediums. Houdini wanted to expose them all as frauds: Doyle always hoped to find one who was genuine.

Doyle died in 1930 at his estate in Eindlesham, England, leaving behind one of the most enduring characters in the world of fiction, the astounding, fascinating Sherlock Holmes.

Other Titles by
Sir Arthur Conan Doyle

The Adventure of the Speckled Band & Other Stories of Sherlock Holmes. New York: New American Library, 1985.

Adventures of Sherlock Holmes. New York: Macmillan, 1985.

Best Supernatural Tales of Arthur Conan Doyle. E. F. Bleiler, editor. New York: Dover Books, 1982.

Case Book of Sherlock Holmes. New York: Berkley Publishing, 1984.

The Complete Sherlock Holmes. New York: Doubleday.

His Last Bow. New York: Berkley Publishing, 1984.

The Hound of the Baskervilles. New York: Dell, 1959.

The Illustrated Sherlock Holmes. New York: Clarkson N. Potter, 1984.

Sherlock Holmes: The Complete Novels and Stories, Vols. I and II. New York: Bantam Books, 1986.

Tales of Terror and Mystery. New York: Penguin, 1989.

Thirty-three by Arthur Conan Doyle. New York: Outlet Book Company, 1986.

The White Company. New York: Buccaneer Books, 1986.